NO DAWN WITHOUT DARKNESS

DAYNA LORENTZ

NO DAWN

WITHOUT DARKNESS

Kathy Dawson Books
AN IMPRINT OF PENGUIN GROUP (USA) LLC

KATHY DAWSON BOOKS

Published by the Penguin Group

Penguin Group (USA) LLC

375 Hudson Street, New York, New York 10014, USA

USA | Canada | UK | Ireland | Australia | New Zealand | India | South Africa | China

penguin.com

A PENGUIN RANDOM HOUSE COMPANY

Library of Congress Cataloging-in-Publication Data

Lorentz, Dayna.

No dawn without darkness : a No safety in numbers book / by Dayna Lorentz.

pages cm

Sequel to: No easy way out.

Summary: "With the power cut and the quarantined mall thrown into darkness, teens Shay, Marco, Lexi, Ryan, and Ginger must change in order to survive, and, when the doors finally open, they may not like what they've become" —Provided by publisher. * ISBN 978-0-8037-3875-1 (hardback) * [1. Interpersonal relations—Fiction. 2. Survival—Fiction. 3. Quarantine—Fiction. 4. Biological warfare—Fiction. 5. Shopping malls—Fiction.] I. Title. * PZ7.L8814Nh 2014   [Fic]—dc23   2013047417

Printed in the U.S.A.

1 3 5 7 9 10 8 6 4 2

Designed by Jason Henry * Text set in Melior

For Joshua

NO DAWN WITHOUT DARKNESS

STONECLIFF SENTINEL

ONLINE EDITION ══════════════════════ *October 28, 20___*

EXPLOSION
AT THE SHOPS AT STONECLIFF?

For the families and friends standing vigil outside the barricade around the Shops at Stonecliff, there was more drama earlier this afternoon.

"It was like an earthquake," stated Hortencia Carvajal, who has been camped outside the mall since her son, Marco, was quarantined inside along with thousands of others two weeks ago. "The ground shifted under me."

A Stonecliff University professor who is studying seismic activity in the region confirmed that his instruments registered a minor shockwave in the area of the Shops at Stonecliff today. "Something on par with the demolition of a small building," Dr. Jorge Kratowski, a professor of geology, explained. "Most likely manmade, given the relatively small amplitude of the wave and its location in a traditionally inactive seismic zone."

Government officials in charge of the quarantined facility refused to comment on the alleged explosion, or the fact that all the lighted signs on the outside of the complex are now off.

This is not the first time family members and friends of those quarantined have felt left in the dark by the government officials managing the facility. Several days ago, thick, black plastic covers were fitted over all the windows in the mall. John Fletcher, Deputy Director of the

Department of Homeland Security and point person for the quarantine management team, stated that the covers were put in place as a precautionary measure after several individuals attempted to escape the facility. Some families on the outside, however, claim that the covers are there to keep them from seeing how bad the conditions inside have become.

There have also been complaints concerning the government's termination of a two-way CB radio system erected earlier in the week to allow family and friends to communicate with their loved ones inside. Though the calls were monitored by the FBI, and were often cut off for no perceptible reason whatsoever, it was still a comfort to be able to speak with those quarantined.

"My ten-year-old son is locked in there with his father," Judy French, another parent standing vigil outside the mall, said. "The man's practically a stranger, he only sees him once a month. Tommy needs to hear his mother's voice."

Deputy Fletcher stated that the CB communication center was terminated as a result of technical difficulties.

The government has repeatedly assured the public during news conferences that they are doing everything in their power to find the person or group responsible for this attack, and that everything inside the mall is safe and secure, that people have access to medical attention, and that there is even a school for the children trapped inside. But with the increasing isolation of those within the mall, and now the darkening of the exterior lights combined with the tremor, how long can the government stay quiet about what's really going on?

DAY
FOURTEEN

GINGER

INSIDE THE STUFF-A-PAL WORKSHOP

am afraid of the dark. I know it seems stupid, one of those kid things everyone grows out of, but I never did.

It's a secret, of course. It's not something you share at the lunch table: *Oh hey guys, you know what? I sleep with THREE night-lights because I'm afraid of the DARK.* There's only one person who knows: my best friend, Maddie. Which is why, when the lights snap off and the floor grumbles and shakes, she squeezes my arm and says, "You're okay."

This is more of a command than a statement of fact. We have not been okay for weeks—not since being trapped with a deadly virus in a mall run by creepy government overlords and psychotic security guards. We are not okay now, huddled on the floor at the back of the Stuff-A-Pal Workshop-turned-jail while all the *nice* men, women, and children are secluded in the HomeMart. Maddie can barely move after having been Tasered by security. My hands are tied together with a strip of plastic that's digging into my skin. But the dark is the worst part. All the noise and shouting stopped, as if the black stole not only the room, but all the people in it. After a heartbeat, the silence turns to screams.

Maybe I am not alone in being afraid of the dark.

Maddie and I keep our backs pressed to the wall. I focus on its solidity against my spine. I need to stay anchored in the darkness: the wall, the floor, Maddie's hand on my arm.

Legs brush past us. My foot is crushed under someone's boot, and the person stumbles, then falls somewhere in front of me. Maddie holds me tighter. Hands grip my hair as they grope for the wall, fingers graze my face. Voices cry out, the gate over the entrance rattles.

A dull lamp flashes on in the hall just outside the store.

Then more lights blink on above my head, off to my right, and above the security gate over the entrance. It's the emergency lighting. Something that makes sense in this world!

Screams turn to cries of joy and spontaneous hugging of strangers. Seconds later, everyone's pushing and shoving their way to the front of the store to bust out the gate.

"Not the gate, morons!" screams some girl next to us in the back. "The stockroom!" She kicks the door Maddie and I were pushed through mere minutes ago. Are there still security guards back there? Would they help even if they were?

"Screw this," a guy at the front yells. He grabs a stool and throws it at the glass display window beside the entrance, but it just bounces off and hits him in the chest. He goes down, disappears in the mass of bodies. I squeeze my back even harder against the wall.

"Remain calm," Maddie whispers through gritted teeth. "I will think of something." But I can tell from her grip on my arm that she is as terrified as I am.

Another guy grabs the stool. This time, he rams the metal legs of the thing against the glass, and it spiderwebs. He kicks out the whole panel. The crowd pours out the new exit into the hallway, and races into the dark. Their howls and cries echo around the cavernous courtyards.

Only when everyone else is gone does Maddie attempt to stand. "I thought that was it," she says, hobbling toward the front. She stares out the gate at the vast blackness beyond. "When the lights went, I thought they were finally ending this thing and blowing us up." A shard of glass drops from the window frame and shatters. "Cowards," Maddie whispers.

She surveys the room, then walks back and holds a hand out to me. "We may as well get the hell out of here."

I let her pull me upright. Until I'm standing, I'm not convinced my legs will carry my weight. Maddie releases me, then flips a switch on the wall—nothing. She hoists herself out the broken front window into the hallway and looks over the balcony at the floors below. People are still screaming. Somewhere, someone's banging on a gate.

"These crappy safety lights are the only ones working in the whole mall," Maddie says, crawling back in through the window and coming to where I stand, frozen. "Government must have cut the power."

"Why would they cut the power?"

She takes a ragged strip of metal from the remains of the stool and begins sawing at the plastic binding my wrists. "Why does that matter?" she says. "It's done. Maybe this is the prelude."

Maddie is convinced that the government wants to blow up the mall with all of us inside it. That this is the only way to keep the virus from getting out and infecting the world.

"They are not going to nuke the place," I say with as much conviction as I can pretend. I cannot believe that after everything we've been through, after how long they've led us to think we can survive this, that they'd just wipe us out.

Maddie slices the last of the plastic, then shrugs. "It's what I'd do."

"So now what?" I ask, moving on.

"We see if there's anything useful under all this crap." Maddie pokes around the store. Like anything of value would remain in the wreckage. The Stuff-A-Pal Workshop has functioned as a jail for days and even in this half-light looks about as good as you'd expect. The foil linings of ripped wrappers glint from every corner. Someone's stained sweatshirt is draped over the register, which lies on the floor in front of the counter. Even the cutesy pictures of cartoon bears and giraffes have been made over with devil horns and buck teeth and . . . other parts. Private parts. Big, hairy private parts, some with faces of their own.

Maddie emerges from a squalid pile with something in her hand, raised like a trophy. "Half a fruit-and-grain bar!" She walks toward me, kicking balls of stuffing across the rug, and splits the bar remnant in two. She holds a piece out to me, shoves the other into her mouth.

"What if the person who ate the rest of that is sick?" I say. "What about germs?" I'm the girl who wipes the rims of shot glasses at parties.

Maddie rolls her eyes, gives me the *oh-honey* look she is so famous for. "Girlfriend, germs fall last on our list of current problems."

I don't agree. At least germs are not last on *my* list. I would rank germs just below the dark, actually. But I will not be able to stay vertical for much longer without some sort of sugar in my body, and so I brush the worst dust and dirt from the surface of the bar, pray that whatever germs were on it are dead, and choke it down.

"We should find a bathroom," Maddie says, digging through more trash and emerging with empty bottles. "And we should fill these, then hunker down until the lights come back on. Or until they blow us up."

"Stop saying that." The one bite of food has made me ravenous. I slide down the wall to my knees and begin rummaging in the trash. There must be another scrap of bar lying around here somewhere.

"And flashlights," Maddie says, continuing her planning. "Crap, those are probably all with the assholes in the HomeMart."

She kicks a trash pile, scattering wrappers. I wonder if there's anything stuck to the insides.

Maddie claps her hands. "Glow sticks!" she says.

"They're practically in every store with Halloween around the cor—" She catches sight of me. "You question my bar, but have no problem licking the inside of a wrapper?"

I start to cry. I don't want to cry. "We're going to die, aren't we?"

Maddie kneels in front of me. "Hey, I'm the Debbie Downer of this duo. You have to be the optimist. Remember, your dad is going to get us out of this. Big Mean Attorney Franklin would never let them blow you up."

I nod. The tears pour down my cheeks.

"Say it," Maddie says.

"Dad will get me out of this."

"Mean it!" Maddie yells, shaking my shoulders.

"My dad would never let me die!"

Maddie smiles. "That's my Ginger."

We carry three empty plastic bottles each to the nearest bathrooms. There is a dim emergency light in the ladies' room, and even in its meager light it's clear the place has returned to its pre-senator-land state: The trash can lies on its side, its contents scattered, and the room smells like the outhouse at my old camp. Why did the senator's nice totalitarian dictatorship have to fall apart? At least under her rules, the bathrooms were cleaned.

At the sink, Maddie pauses before turning the handle.

Water sputters forth. She lets out a little bark of a laugh. "We have water!" she cries.

There was a chance we wouldn't have water?

"Start filling," she commands.

I obey.

We fill the bottles, then take a moment to wash our

faces and hands. Maddie ducks into the dark of a stall. I gulp water straight from the faucet. It's almost as good as eating.

"Where'd you get those bottles?"

I lift my head from the sink and see a guy in the doorway. He looks like a college kid, but that could just be the Harvard T-shirt. In other circumstances, he might seem cute.

"We found them," Maddie says. She stands inside the door to her stall.

"Looks to me like you have a spare one," he says, walking toward me.

My heart races. I grip the edge of the sink. His eyes glint in the dim light like some animal's. We have six bottles. Do we need all six?

"These are our bottles," Maddie says. "Scrounge your own."

The guy keeps walking toward me. "At least let me get a drink."

Maddie steps in front of him. "Use the men's room."

The guy puts his hands on Maddie's shoulders, like he's going to shove her aside. She leans in, grabs his sleeves, pulls him toward her, and smashes his nuts with her knee. The guy drops to the floor.

"Stupid bitch!" he yelps, holding his groin. "I just want a drink!"

Maddie grabs her three bottles. "Then you should have used the men's room." She shoves my bottles at me. "Let's go."

"Should we tell someone he's in there?" I ask.

Maddie stops mid-stride and faces me. "Stop worrying about him. Stop worrying about anyone else. This," she says, pointing from her face to mine, "is all we worry about." She grabs my arm and drags me along behind her.

"We will get killed if we try to get food now," Maddie says. We stare over the railing at the mob raiding the Sam's Club. It's like a mosh pit, only the people are fighting over canned goods, not dancing.

"Let's snag us some glow sticks," she says, heading toward the stalled escalator.

The third floor looks abandoned. Maddie darts across the hall to the costume place, Shades of Halloween. I lope behind her. She stops at a display of glow wands and necklaces and cleans out the whole thing into her gargantuan purse.

"Go check the stockroom," she snaps over her shoulder as she moves on to the next display.

"Is it a good idea to split up?"

"There's no one here," Maddie says. "Go now before that changes."

Shades of Halloween is not a regular store for obvious reasons—every season, the space morphs into something else: "Shades of Halloween" to "Down Home Christmas" to "Blooming Bunnies" and so on. There's little back in the stockroom, which makes sense. Why stock a lot of stuff if the store is only around for a few months?

I find one locked door. Maddie will kill me if I return empty-pursed, so I ransack the checkout counter and find a key ring marked SPARE rattling around in the back of the bottommost drawer. Three keys into the ring, the door opens to reveal a closet packed with candy.

A laugh escapes my lips. Of course the closet is packed with candy.

When I was five, Maddie's mom took me trick-or-treating for the first time. Maddie was a brown dog and I was a ballerina, dressed in one of my mom's old tutus. Coming home, my bag was so full of candy, I could hardly lift it up the stoop. Mom took my bag as she closed the door behind me. *I can't believe she lets Maddie eat this poison,* she said as she dumped my whole sack into the trash. Then she smoothed a stray hair back into my bun. *Serious dancers don't pollute their bodies with junk food.* I wanted to be a serious dancer like her, so I never ate candy. Ever. Until now.

I tear a bag of Snickers open, pick out a mini bar, unwrap it, and bite.

It's so sweet, I gag. Then I eat the whole bar in a single swallow. And another. And another.

"You trying to make yourself sick?"

I freeze mid-bite and turn to face Maddie. "I was hungry," I manage.

Maddie snatches the bag from my hands and jams it into my purse. "Let's start you slow on the sugar, okay?"

She fills both our purses, then shuts the door and locks it, stowing the keys in her pocket. "This will be our stash," she says. "Let them eat chocolate!"

"Marie Antoinette died, you know." The sugar is beginning to course through my veins. I feel like my head might explode.

"But not from starvation," Maddie says, shaking a Snickers at me.

Something crashes out in the store. Maddie peers out the narrow window in the stockroom door, then holds a finger to her lips. I creep to her side.

There's a group of people, guys and girls, rummaging around. They look older, but it's hard to tell in the dim light from the one emergency bulb above the door. Is it me, or has the light dimmed?

"We should all wear the same mask," one says. He holds up a gorilla head.

"Masks are dumb," says another guy by the registers. "You can't see anything."

"Who cares if we can see?" a girl says from the other end of the store. "The emergency lights are already running out of power. It's going to be completely dark again in a few hours."

"The point is to identify our group," says register guy— make that claw guy. His knuckles sparkle, like he's wearing a fistful of rings, but the rings are all topped with curved knives. Whatever fear I had ticks up a notch.

The girl pulls out a black hooded dress, like what the Grim Reaper would wear. "This. We all wear this, but wrap tape from the post office around our arms."

"We'd blend into the dark," gorilla-mask guy says, shrugging. "How is this different than doing nothing?"

Claw guy abandons his post, examines the costume. "Doing nothing, we look like everyone else." He grabs one of the robes off the rack, pulls something off the makeup display, and shoves it into the gorilla guy's chest. "We'll put this on our faces to stand out," he says, and returns to the door. "Let's move."

Gorilla guy opens the package and smears his cheeks with slashes of glow-in-the-dark paint. "Hells yeah."

When they're gone, Maddie makes a beeline for the Grim Reaper rack and tugs one of the robes over her head. She grabs a second and shoves it into my chest.

"Why are we putting on their costume?"

"Because then, if they find us, they might think we're with them and leave us alone. Also, it hides our bags. No one will know we have supplies."

"Why would anyone bother us?" I ask, pulling the thin, itchy cloth over my head.

"Why wouldn't they?"

Maddie seems to think the people in the mall are going to start turning on one another. I don't believe it. The guy in the bathroom just wanted a drink. Yes, security went crazy, but the people left in here are just regular kids. Once things calm down—

The emergency lights in the store flicker, then die.

The world is black again.

A hand grabs my arm. "We have to hide."

It's Maddie.

I let her lead me through the dark.

RYAN

INSIDE THE SHOE HUT

I f the main lights are out it means security has bigger problems than watching this crap jail. I've got to get out of here and look for Shay. I won't leave the one person I care about alone in this hellhole.

When dull, yellow emergency lights come on, I head for the locked stockroom door. But everyone else has the same idea. I'm crushed against a shelf. The first guy to reach the door starts slamming his shoulder into the wood until it cracks and he breaks through. The crowd presses forward, smashing my face into a shelf of men's dress shoes.

Enough.

I throw an elbow, then execute a tuck-and-roll—arms in, spin out—to get around this jerk who's trying to pin me. But once free, there's nowhere to go. It's solid bodies from me to the lead guy, who's stuck in the door.

People claw the guy, push him deeper into the wood panel. He screams, then disappears through the hole into the stockroom.

The crowd surges ahead. I'm shoved through by the force of the people behind me. My shoe gets caught against what remains of the door and I'm pinned down. Wood bites into a cut on my ankle.

I'm stuck, but then the pressure shifts and I jerk my leg, scraping the skin against the splinters, the pain so bad I see stars. Then my shoe pops off and my foor flops to the floor. I army-crawl across the narrow strip of tile, away from the flood of people headed for a set of double doors into the service hallway.

My ankle looks like crap. I pull out the bits of wood, but the skin all the way to the bottom of my foot is completely messed up.

Once the crowd is gone, I find my shoe, jam my foot into it, and wedge myself between a stool and the wall to lever my body to standing. I test the ankle. It holds. Sort of.

I take a step. It feels like a knife being jammed through my foot.

I've never had an injury I couldn't play through. Concussions, sprained everything, even a chipped tibia—I kept going. This ankle is nothing.

I try again.

It takes five attempts before I'm convinced. I'm not going anywhere.

I drag myself into the deepest shadow I can find and lay my head back. Even if I found Shay now, what good would I be to her?

■   ■   ■

"Got a live one," a woman's voice says, followed by the squeal of a walkie-talkie. She's in a black security uniform, and a stun stick hangs from her belt. "You okay?"

"I'm fine," I say.

She snorts. "You might be fine, but that ankle's toast. I'm Tina Skelton," she says, holding out her hand. "I promise, I don't bite."

Not having much of a choice, I grab her hand and let her haul me up. She digs her shoulder under mine to keep me standing. She's surprisingly strong.

"I have a first aid kit back at the pet store," she says, taking a step. "I'll fix that foot good as new."

"Why are you helping me?" I ask.

She looks confused by the question. "Don't you need help?"

Tina lugs me down the service hall to the pet store. The back room is lit by a few dim emergency lights, which glint off the eyes and wet noses of the dogs caged along the walls. When they see us, they get all excited and start jumping and wagging their tails.

"Calm it down, kids!" Tina says, smiling at the cages. "I took care of them. Senator Ross didn't worry about the animals, but me, I'm a dog person. How about you?"

"I was never allowed to have a pet," I say as Tina eases me into a chair.

"Well, now you have ten."

She closes the door to the main part of the store, then opens the cages. The puppies race out across the floor, yipping and wiggling their whole bodies. One little black guy licks my hand over and over, nipping my fingers with his sharp, spikey teeth.

"Knew you had a smile in there," Tina says, winking at me.

She sits on the desk beside me and lifts my bad ankle. She dabs it with hydrogen peroxide, then smears on protective cream. Her fingers are warm and fat, nothing like my mom's, but it still feels nice.

Tina pulls a thick roll of gauze from her bag and slowly wraps my ankle. I lift my hand and pet the dog's head. My eyes swell up and leak, and my nose gets going.

"Allergic?" Tina asks, handing me a box of tissues.

"No," I say, and wipe my face clean.

"Skelton!" a man's voice shouts, waking me.

I'm dozing in the dog bed with Tuffer—the little black puppy. Tina gave me some Tylenol, and between it and the ankle, I was out. I'm not sure for how long, but it was long enough for the emergency lights to dim to nothing.

Tina appears from a back office with a flashlight. "Hold your water, Hank!"

Hank. Hank Goldman.

I grab on to the nearest desk and drag myself up. Tina's wrap is good and tight, so I can almost put weight on the ankle.

"Where you going?" she asks, pointing the flashlight at me and opening the door into the main store.

Too late. Goldman walks in with two other security guys and I am screwed.

"I see we have a visitor," Goldman says, striding toward me. He's got a flashlight of his own and it's blinding. "If it isn't Jimmy Murphy's kid."

"You know him?" Tina asks.

"Everyone knows him. This is Spider-Kid!" Goldman is inches from my face. "He ran with a pretty tough crowd. You know anything about our little power problem?"

"Leave him alone," Tina says, shoving her way between us. "Even if he had friends, he doesn't anymore. I found him alone with a busted ankle in the back of the Shoe Hut."

Goldman's breath reeks of onions. My mouth waters.

"If he was jailed in the Shoe Hut," Tina continues, "there's no way he was involved with the blackout. Now tell me what you're doing out of the HomeMart."

"Senator has me on one of her errands," says Goldman. "I was kicked out with an electrician to investigate the cause of this blackout. Turns out, someone pierced the transformer, blowing the whole mall's electrical system apart. The thing can't be fixed.

"Coming back, we were rushed by some kids and I lost the electrician. When I finally got to the HomeMart, it didn't matter anyway. The senator's gotten cute. Says she won't let me or anyone else back in without her kid. Marshall and Kearns caught up with me on my way here." Goldman sits, picks up my dog. He pats him like he's his.

"That woman," Tina says, shaking her head. "I'm not sure what we'll do until we find the girl. We have a sink that works, but the only food back here is dog kibble."

"We're never going to find that girl." Goldman puts down my dog and examines a giant bag of kibble. "But I think we can eat better than this."

His plan is simple extortion. Goldman will wait until the kids have scavenged the Sam's Club clean, then he'll hit up anyone he finds for a protection fee. "No doubt they're waking up to the fact that the biggest thing they have to fear now is each other." He points to the bag. "We can sweeten the deal, maybe offer protection plus kibble."

"And if they don't give you their food?" Tina says.

"We zap them."

"Why not just go in zapping?" Marshall asks.

"You have an extra cartridge I don't know about?" Goldman says. "I used my last one getting here. And I don't want to have to get in close. No telling what these"— he glances at me—"*animals* will do."

He pulls the gun from his belt and holds it out to Marshall. "I go in first, negotiate with the bastards. If any of them make a move, wing them with this."

Kearns says the Sam's Club has cleared, so he, Marshall, and Goldman head out to shake down teenagers.

"Seems crazy," Tina says, standing her flashlight on its end so it dimly lights the room. She sits and the dogs pile on her. "I wish I could say the man's wrong, but most of these kids? They're trouble."

"Why'd you help me?"

She holds Tuffer up to me, and I cradle him against my chest. "You looked like good people," she says.

If only she knew. A week ago, she would have left me for dead.

"See?" She points to Tuffer. "Dogs know good people too."

The stupid puppy squirms to lick my face, and I loosen my arms so he can, the little idiot.

The door from the service hall slams open. A bright white light clicks on.

It's a kid my age. "Dude, it's just one old lady," he says

to someone behind him. He's wearing a headlamp and holding a metal baseball bat smeared with blood. "Marco's nuts."

He's from Mike's gang.

Tina hops to her feet, brandishing her stun stick; the dogs scatter. "Security's holding this location, so you'd better move on."

"See? It *is* security. Just like Marco said." A girl's voice.

Two other headlamps click on. The girl and another guy. I drop to the floor, press my back to the desk to hide. Tuffer yelps and slips from my arms.

"My bad," the first guy says. "Okay, lady. You give us that stick and the radio, and we'll let you clear out."

"You kids just find a place to hole up until we can sort this power situation out."

"What's to sort out?" the girl asks. "We blew the power."

"Now hand them over like a nice security hack," the first guy says.

"I will not ask you to leave again."

Feet scuffle. The bat cracks against Tina's stun stick. Glancing around the corner of the desk, I see the flash of a blade. The girl has a knife and goes for Tina's gut. Tina kicks her in the knee, the girl topples. The second guy comes at Tina with a machete. She gets her stun stick in front of her, but the blow glances off and hits her arm.

Tina stumbles back, lifts her walkie-talkie. "Home base!" she screams.

The guys are on her again. She Tases one, dropping him like a bag, and smacks another in the head. They're coming closer.

I crawl around the desk toward where I saw Tina come

out of the back office, then, finding the door open, crawl into the dark.

Tina screams. "Help!" But there are three of them, and I can't walk, can barely crawl. I can't help anything. I'd only get myself killed.

Tina cries out. Something hit her hard. She screams again, then is silent.

"You see someone else in here?"

"Yo, flashlights outside!"

"Grab Pierce!"

Footsteps, the door slamming against the wall again, then silence. The light drops down to just Tina's flashlight.

I crawl out of the office. Tina is on the ground. Her eyes are open, vacant. My arms shake. Tuffer pads out of the dark and licks her cheek.

I am what I always knew I was—the coward crouched in the corner behind Thad, watching my father hit him, just hoping Dad tired out before my brother went down.

"Skelton!" Goldman shouts. "Tina!" His flashlight shines in the store.

He'll think I did this. I as good as did this.

My only thought is to run. I try to stand. Pain throbs from the ankle, but it holds and I hobble out, taking the same route as the killers.

The hall is so dark, it's like I've disappeared, and that's perfect, because all I want to be is nothing.

GINGER

INSIDE THE STOCKROOM OF
SHADES OF HALLOWEEN

Time is meaningless in the black. I feel like we've been sitting here for hours. Our hands groping for walls, knobs, carts, obstacles, anything, we slowly found our way to what felt like a safe corner to hunker down in and wait. For what, I don't know.

I hear a wrapper crinkle beside me.

"Should I eat too?" I am this lost—I have to ask permission to snack.

"Eat, don't eat," Maddie says. "I'm not sure it matters."

"I'm having another Snickers."

Maddie cracks a glow stick, shakes it, and pink light blooms in front of my face. Oh god, I missed light. My eyes tear up and blur the bright wand into a brilliant haze.

"Thank you," I manage, choking on a sob.

"Home sweet stockroom," she says. "At least we're better off than the people out there."

"Like Lexi?" I ask. Before the lights went out, we were supposed to rescue her. We failed.

"I'm sure she's safe with her senator mom in the Home-Mart." Maddie pops several Skittles into her mouth. "She probably has a nice bed, real food, a lantern."

She throws the wrapper at the wall, goes digging in her bag for another packet, then freezes. "Holy crap," she says. Her hand emerges with a walkie-talkie. "I totally forgot I had this!"

The senator gave it to us so we could call when we found Lexi. She'd promised to keep us all safe in the HomeMart.

Maddie turns it on and the thing squeals. We both freak and try to smother it. Maddie regains brain power first and winds down the volume.

We listen for a while, but all the conversations are in code—team numbers but never names, fake locations like "home base" and "red cave." I wonder why they would be using codes to talk to other security guards. Maybe we're not the only non-security people with a working walkie-talkie. Then we hear:

All teams have reported back except two and eleven. A man's voice. *I lost the electrician coming up from the garage.*

Did anyone find my daughter? The senator.

We have a little more to worry about than one lost kid.

Maddie turns off the radio. "We have to find Lexi."

"We couldn't find her when the lights were on," I say. "It's crazy to think we could find her now." I cannot go back out into the dark.

"I'm not okay leaving her alone out there," Maddie says, standing.

She can't leave me. "What does it matter if the government's just going to blow us up?" I can't believe I said it.

Maddie jams the walkie-talkie into her bag. "It matters because that's what friends do."

A creak—the door.

"There!" a guy's voice cries. "It's a light!"

Maddie drops and sits on our glow stick.

"Where?" Another voice—a girl.

"In the corner," the guy says. "Two people, I think. They're wearing capes."

Maddie slips a hand over my mouth.

"We don't want to hurt you," the girl says. "We came looking for glow sticks. Please, give us one. Just one. Then we'll go."

Footsteps. They are coming toward us.

I hear a crash, then swearing.

"Where are you?"

"Here! I hurt my knee."

"Is this you?"

"Get off my face!"

I want to help them. I want to throw a glow stick—all the glow sticks at them. *Just go away! Leave us alone in our corner.*

"We don't want to hurt you!" the guy yells. "Please, just one stick."

I stay silent and still.

Maddie moves, something rustles. Green light bursts forth, then flies. The glow stick hits the wall, then lands.

"Thank god!" the girl cries. The green light lifts. Lights a face. Glints off the wet trails of tears on her skin.

Then I feel a hand on my foot.

"Now give us another."

I kick my legs, drive my feet into a body. All instinct, no thought.

The guy wraps his arms around my legs, crawls his fingers up my body. I punch him. He grunts, takes the blows. Maddie releases my mouth.

"Get off me!" I scream, grabbing at hair, eyes, ears—pushing them away.

"What are you doing, Gav?" the girl cries to her partner.

Then there's a blur of pink light and the smash of something hard hitting something harder. The guy falls still, head in my lap.

"Gavin!" the girl screams. The green light comes toward us.

Maddie drops the pink glow stick and broken pieces of walkie-talkie, swings her bag, and nails the girl in the head. The girl's body hits the ground with a thud.

"Stop it!" I scream, referring to everyone, though only Maddie is listening. I drag my butt along the floor, away from the guy's body. His head slides over my thigh, then thunks onto the cement.

"I should have known," Maddie mutters, slinging her bag over her cassock. "I can't believe I was that stupid." She bends to pick up the green glow stick. Her hand is shaking. "This is not a freaking charity event."

Maddie shoves the green glow stick into my chest, and marches toward the door leading into the service halls. "We go right," she says.

I shuffle along until I can catch a corner of her sleeve in my claw.

She looks back at me like she's going to punch me.

"Please," I yelp.

She pulls me into a hug. "You have seen my self-defense skills," she says. "And yet you still think it's wise to sneak up and grab me?" She kisses my head, then tows me along.

There are a few emergency lights still burning in the service halls. Maddie won't let me linger by them. She says they are too dangerous. "People can see you," she whispers, "but you can't see them."

How is stumbling through the dark with firefly-level lighting in our hands any less dangerous?

Maddie stops and tests the first door handle. "Unlocked," she mutters. "All the magnetic doors must be unlocked." The door is marked CLAIRE'S. "Did we check here before?" she asks.

"Maybe," I say. After escaping security's attack on the IMAX, we ran down the maze of service hallways, then searched around the arcade. Who knows what stores we missed?

"Then let's check it out," she says, and we enter, glow sticks first.

The first thing my glow stick illuminates is a dead body.

I scream. Maddie punches my arm. I stop screaming.

We roll the body over. It's a boy. He smells god-awful. Blood dribbles from his mouth, nose, and eyes. His skin is weirdly dark, like patches have been blacked out. I step over him, grab the edge of a shelf, and throw up Snickers bits and bile.

"He's not even cold," Maddie says. What possessed her to touch him?

"Wipe off your hands," I say, thrusting hand sanitizer at her.

"I already had the flu."

"Just wipe them." I haven't had the flu. Plus the virus has mutated now. Maybe Maddie can get it again. I'd like for us to not end up like this guy.

When she hands it back to me, I rub a small amount of the stuff over my face and hands. It stings my eyes, but what's a little pain compared with ending up an oozing obstacle on a stockroom floor?

We poke around the junk in the stockroom, but there's no sign of Lexi. I don't even know what a sign of Lexi would look like.

"Ready to call it?" I ask.

"Let's check the store." Maddie heads for the exit into the store proper.

I got my ears pierced with Maddie and her mom at a Claire's when I was ten. My dad was furious. He pulled the studs out and let the holes close up. Then, when I was thirteen, he took me to a "nice place" and had real diamond-and-gold studs put in. Of course, I had a reaction to the fancy earrings, and had to switch to the cheap, surgical steel ones I'd gotten years before at Claire's.

The store is narrow and crowded with merchandise. Apparently, the senator's society had no use for Hello Kitty costume jewelry and faux-silk scarves. Further emphasizing the store's uselessness is the fact that the security gate is pulled down over the entrance to the mall.

The screams and shouts we'd heard in the stockroom are louder here. The cavernous black of the main mall echoes with voices.

"Get that guy! He's got a flashlight!"

"She stole a bag of nuts!"

"Get the boys together—I found some kids with a stash of batteries."

"Hey! That's my bag!"

"Get her!"

"Get him!"

"Get them!"

The space between the shouts is filled with slapping footsteps and the squealing shoe soles.

Flashlight beams cut through the black like a laser show, sometimes catching a fleeing person, sometimes simply glinting off the windows, sometimes hitting a mirror and sending sparks of light all over. Multicolored glow sticks, glow necklaces, and glow wands wink in the shadows or streak by in a blur. Down on the first floor, someone has lined the rim of the central fountain with candles. A bright orange blaze from an unseen corner on the third floor suggests others have sabotaged the sprinkler system and actually built bonfires. Even with this, the majority of the place is still black, black, black.

"Lexi?" Maddie says, then coughs. "The air tastes stale." She pulls out her inhaler, gives it a shake. "Not good."

"Do you feel an attack?" Sixth grade, in gym, Maddie's breathing got so bad, the teacher brought in an oxygen mask.

"No," she says. "But without air-conditioning, I doubt the air is going to get better." She takes out a water bottle and sips. "Figures I survive the killer flu only to die from asthma."

Die? Why is she talking about dying? "You said you're fine."

"Now," she said. "But one more bonfire, and I'm going to be hacking up a lung."

"What is it, the smoke?" I ask. I'm sort of yelling because that's better than sort of crying. I rack my brain for the information handed out in those elementary school presentations by the fire department. Stay low to the ground. Cover your mouth with a wet cloth.

"Let's get face masks," I say. "From the med center. On the first floor."

Maddie watches the craziness out in the halls. "We have to find Lexi," she says, gripping the links of the gate.

I grab Maddie's shoulders and turn her to face me. "You can't help her if you can't breathe." I straighten the strap on her bag, then pull up the hood of her cassock. "We are going to the goddamned med center."

Maddie smirks, then gives a little salute, shoulders squared. "Yes, sir!"

"Help!"

Someone crashes into the security gate. We stumble back and hit a display, sending beads bouncing everywhere.

It's a guy. He rattles the links. "Let me in!"

Neither Maddie nor I move. We hide our glow sticks in our sleeves and pretend to be shadows.

"I've got him!" Another boy materializes from the black. He has a headlamp on, like he's camping. More boys with headlamps surround the pathetic kid. They tug his hands loose from the gate, pull off his coat, and begin shaking out the pockets.

"You could let me keep a bag of chips," the pathetic guy cries. Two headlamps have his arms and hold him still.

One of the headlamps is this guy I met early on in the quarantine: Mike. Egomaniac football player, a senior at one of the local high schools. We kind of hooked up, but he kissed like he was trying to bite my face off.

"Cleaned him out?" A tall kid in a duster coat steps forward, bends down, and picks through the loot. All beams are on him.

"It's Marco," Maddie whispers.

Marco's with the headlamp gang? It looks like his face got messed up. One side is red and oozy, like he tried to burn it off.

"What should we do with him?" Mike asks—wait, *Mike* asks *Marco*?

Holy crap. Marco—scrawny, geeky, video-game-playing, nerdy-movie-quoting Marco—is the *leader* of the headlamp gang?

"Toss him," Marco says. "He won't try to steal our stash again."

The headlamps gather the stuff they picked off the guy and slink away down the hall.

The pathetic guy is dropped into the black. "Thanks for the help," he says. The gate rattles. "Hello? I know you're in there."

The gate will protect us. "What do you want?" I squeak. Maddie elbows me in the side.

"Food, water," he says, sounding almost jokey, "a nice place on Fire Island for the summer. You have any of the above?"

I pull out a Snickers and throw it at the gate. "Here." I feel sorry for him. He doesn't seem bad.

"Did you just throw food, water, or a very small beach hut?" The gate rattles.

But I've been the worst judge of bad, so I clamp down on that sorry feeling and hold on tighter to Maddie. "What should we do?" I whisper.

Maddie elbows me again. "What's it like out there?" she asks him.

"Oh, it's a picnic in the park." The gate rattles again, then a bright white light flashes on. I'm blinded by its brilliance. Then the light goes out. We hear a wrapper crinkle. "Oh, god, chocolate has never tasted so good."

"What was that light?" Maddie asks.

It flashes on again, this time illuminating his face. He is totally hot. And older. Like maybe twenty-five. He has long eyelashes that curl over soulful eyes. He is, like, the definition of my type. Then the light is gone again.

"It's a book light," he says. "I keep this puppy hidden on my person to avoid losing it in such shakedowns as you girls just witnessed. Thanks for the help, by the way."

"What would you have liked us to do?" Maddie says. "We can't open that gate. And even if we could have, it's not like we're looking to hang with thieves."

He leans against the gate, causing it to creak. "Girlfriend," he says, "thieving is all we've got left." He offers to share his tale of woe for two more Snickers. This sounds like a good deal to me, so I toss two more at the gate. Once he locates them with his light, he continues.

His name is Kris. "When the lights went out, I was hiding in Baxter's Books. I left the store, and came across those headlamp nutbags in the bowling alley just sitting on a huge pile of grub. We're talking jerky, pretzels, trail mix in little bags." He takes a moment. "Anyway, they chased me over here and now you know as much as I."

Maddie is frozen against the table, arms crossed over her chest. I slide down to the floor, to his level. I would feed him all my food if he would just turn on that light again.

"How could the headlamp people have gotten so much food, and hauled it all the way up to the bowling alley?" Maddie asks, still sounding wary.

"Before the blackout, a bunch of lunatics armed to the teeth took on a food caravan guarded by security. Security was trying to move the food into the HomeMart before it was locked down. The headlamp people must have been with the lunatics. Which suggests they have weapons. Maybe I shouldn't have tried stealing from them first."

I crawl to the gate. "Please turn on your light," I say, holding out a Snickers.

Just when he's about the grab it, he snatches at my bag instead.

Maddie kicks the gate, knocking his hand loose, and drags me back. "Ginger!" she scolds.

He laughs. "Oh, come now," he says. "I won't bite. Okay, I might bite, but I'm just starving. There's been no food service for, god, how long? A day? And how many packets of madeleine cookies from the bookstore coffee shop can you eat?" He turns on the light—a peace offering? "Actually, I can tell you exactly how many—fifteen. Then you begin to hate madeleines."

"Was there a girl with the headlamps?" Maddie asks. "A black girl, kind of curvy? With the burned guy, the leader?"

Kris flashes his light at us. "I don't know. There were a bunch of them there. We could go check," he says. "I'll show you where they're hiding for a bag of candy."

"No need," Maddie says. "I'm sure we can find the bowling alley ourselves."

"Suit yourself," he mutters, shrugging. "But you sure you don't want a hulking male presence along to defend you?"

Kris is far from a hulking male presence. Even Maddie cracks a smile.

"I think we'll do all right on our own," she says.

"Best of luck, then." He flicks off his light. I hear the gate clatter, then footsteps. We are alone again.

"You think Lexi's with the headlamps?" I ask, shuffling in the dark.

"Marco's face was burned," she says. "Maybe he was in the IMAX when the tear gas exploded. And maybe Lex was there with him. We didn't exactly scour the place before security busted in—" She's cut off by a wracking cough.

"First, we get face masks," I say.

She nods and takes another sip.

DAY
—
FIFTEEN

THE SENATOR

AUDIO LOG

Left on a machine using a satellite phone and a pre-arranged phone number:

This is Dorothy Ross calling with my report on the status inside the mall, in accordance with your order after the loss of internal and external monitoring due to the power outage. I had expected to speak with someone directly. Maybe I got the time wrong? Please confirm my call-in times for the future.

We have approximately five hundred people packed in the HomeMart—adults and young children. The temperature is seventy-five degrees; last night it was seventy-two.

As requested, I sent my chief of security, Hank Goldman, out with John Dawes, an electrician, to investigate the power situation. They made it to the transformer, but found it had been damaged beyond repair. Mr. Dawes suggested that the transformer would not have exploded on its own. Mr. Goldman readily supported his claim that this was deliberate sabotage. I have not had further reports from Misters Goldman or Dawes, nor have they returned to the HomeMart.

I have collected all batteries and hand-crank generators, light sources, and walkie-talkies. What power we have will be directed toward maintaining the walkie-talkies and this satellite phone, then to the light sources.

We have food, though not enough. I have ordered the remaining members of security to divide what we have into rations, giving the most to the children. By some blessing, the plumbing still works, so we have water, and there are bathrooms and a staff kitchen in the store.

I have asked all the adults to pitch in to keep the store clean, including maintaining the bathrooms. The HomeMart is conveniently well-stocked with cleaning materials.

I have limited information about the conditions in the rest of the mall. From what I hear through the locked security gate, which is solid like a garage door, the situation has descended into chaos. I have not heard further reports from Dr. Chen, and assume that he has either succumbed to illness or been compromised in some other way. He was not able to update me on the progress of his research before all communication was cut off.

Please call me back to update me on your timeline for the situation. In particular as to whether you have decided to go forward with Project Closed Book. I fear the news about Dr. Chen decides the matter. I would like to be informed before you destroy the mall with me and everyone I love inside it.

R
Y
A
N

INSIDE THE POST OFFICE

Wake up!" a guy yells, then slaps my face.

I block, too late, and scurry back, away from the hand. Last thing I remember, I was running from Goldman. He was yelling that he'd kill me. Then two people with glowing green heads jumped me.

My eyes are blurred out by the light. I'm somewhere with power.

"I don't know why you brought him back here," the guy says. The voice is familiar.

"Giles punched him," a girl says. "I didn't want to just leave him out there."

"Last time I saw him, he attacked us." A new guy—Giles, I bet. "Better safe than sorry."

"Bet your ass," the first guy says. "And Diane, no more

bringing home strays. We are not running a goddamned shelter."

This room is the back of the post office and this guy is the leader of the post office gang—Simon, I think. The ceiling lights are out, so I was wrong about there being power, but with all the flashlights and lanterns hung everywhere, it's as bright as it was the last time I was here, three days ago. With Shay.

"The girl I was with," I say.

"He speaks!" Simon says.

"Did she come here?"

Simon throws Shay's universal key card at me. "Traded information on the whereabouts of her sister for this, which is useless now that all the service hall doors are open."

Out of nowhere, a guy in a hooded sweatshirt steps forward. "Where is she?"

"Who let this guy in?" Simon yells, brandishing his fist of knives and grabbing the guy's arm.

The postal people are on the intruder in a second. One pulls back his hood. It's Kris. Shay's co-teacher. The guy who hates me.

Kris puts his hands up. "I'm just looking for Shay," he says. "Tell me where you sent her and I'll get lost."

Diane frisks him and pulls a bag of chips from his pocket. "He stole food."

"Borrowed," Kris says. "Just borrowing."

Simon throws his arms up. "What the hell did we set up patrols for? Where are my door guards?" He grabs the chips and hurls the bag across the room. "What the hell are we doing here, people?!" Simon picks up a tablet and begins reading from a list. "Jake, Liz—door duty. Diane, Giles—first patrol. We have a system, people. This is the way we've survived."

A girl plays with the zipper on her hoodie. "I had to go to the bathroom."

"And you let in a thief," Simon says, slamming the tablet down. "I want two people per door at all times from now on."

Another girl, the one who caught Shay and me— Sydney—nods and takes the tablet.

The postal people tape Kris's hands behind his back, then toss him beside me, under a wide shelf, between boxes and a huge canvas bin of trash.

He's got a black eye. It makes him look less like a pretty-boy actor. "Who gave you that?" I ask.

"Your pals Mike and Marco," he says. "Thanks for leaving me, by the way."

Last time I saw Kris, he was helping me get a little girl named Ruthie into the HomeMart. Once we got her inside I had to ditch Kris because Mike's gang ambushed the security team's food caravan and I saw my old teammate Drew go down in the fight.

"I thought my friend had been shot," I say. "But it was the flu."

"You're better off without them," Kris says. He shuffles toward one of the legs of the shelving unit and begins rubbing the tape holding his wrists against the edge.

I can't argue. When I left Mike, he had a gun pointed to my face.

The postal people huddle in the opposite corner. From

what I can hear, Simon is tearing them a new one over their failure to take security seriously. My arms are free. There's nothing holding me down except my ankle. They can tell just by looking at me that I'm no threat.

The tape cuffing Kris snags, and he tugs his arms apart until it splits. He then crawls, slowly, toward the edge of the shelf, slides his hand onto the top, and feels around. "Gotcha." He brings his hand back down, holding a thin laptop.

"Saw it while they were taping me up." Kris opens it and begins clicking through windows. "We can find Shay. Here we are." It's a database of names, ages, whether someone's sick or dead, and current check-ins. Kris scrolls down to Dixit. Next to Shay's sister's name, it says *JCPenney.*

That's where Shay went. She could still be there.

He looks at me. "Coming?"

Shay would come for me, no question. Hurt, sick, out-gunned, she'd be there.

I could play defense between Shay and an attacker. Even broken, I could at least do that.

I try to stand and hit my head.

"Slow down, champ. We need a plan," Kris says, slipping the computer back where he found it. "There's a door over there." He points past the garbage bin.

I get my knees under me. "That's our plan," I say. I crawl over, then jam myself between the bin and the wall. Kris positions his arms behind the other corner of the bin, and on my nod, we shove the whole thing over, sending weeks' worth of trash spilling across the room.

Simon whips his head around. "Was no one watching them? What the hell have we just been talking about?" he screams, and the whole group of them comes charging.

Kris pulls open the door. I scramble up, using the wall as a crutch, and hobble to him.

"You have to move faster than that," he says, glancing over my shoulder at the advancing line of postal people wading through the foot-deep pile of crap.

There's a brick by the door that must have been some kind of doorstop when this place was still functioning. I heft it, then slam it down on the inside door handle, which pops off the door and into my hand. I step into the service hall and then shut the door.

"Where'd you get that idea?" Kris asks.

One night, my dad got fed up with some stupid fight Thad and I were having over a video game. My dad hauled us up to our room, and to keep us in there, he busted the doorknob. Thad crawled out the window, just to stick it to the old man.

"Just came to me," I say.

Kris flips on a book light. "I keep this *well* hidden," he says, smiling. I do not want to know where.

Next to us are the smooth metal doors of an elevator. I wedge the door handle into the seam and wrench the elevator doors apart far enough to get my fingertips in.

"I don't think the elevator's working," Kris says.

"The postal people expect us to come out the service halls on this side," I say. "No way I can outrun them." The doors slide open onto the empty shaft. "They won't expect us to change floors."

Kris shines his light into the elevator shaft. I guessed right. Just like in that movie, there's an emergency ladder on one wall.

The elevator car is above us. "We're going down," Kris says.

He helps me get onto the rungs, then slides the doors shut behind us.

It's a slow climb down. Kris stops at the first floor, but I shake my head.

"Parking level."

"It's got to be pitch-black down there," he says.

"Security controls the first floor."

He nods, keeps descending. Seems he's aware that security is the enemy. We drop onto the floor of the shaft, push the release on the doors, and crawl into the black of the parking level.

We're near where they built the showers. The air feels damp, and it smells like mildew. Kris scans around with his light, but it gets lost in the huge, black space.

"JCPenney's on the other side," he says, and we begin picking our way across the mall.

I have to lean on Kris after a few steps. We move even slower. He's no athlete.

"Can't you put *any* weight on that leg?" he grunts.

"I *am* putting weight on it," I snap.

A door opens somewhere nearby. We stop. Beams of light swing around.

"Headlamps," Kris says. "Crap." He turns off his light.

A voice echoes, "I think the bikes were parked somewhere over here." It's the guy from the pet store.

"You have to hotwire them or can we just roll them?" Mike's voice.

No thought, just instinct, forgetting everything except Mike's gun in my face and Tina's dead eyes, I bolt. I get one step before my ankle gives out and I fall onto a car. The alarm blares. Headlights flash.

Kris grabs me, hauls me up. "Nice move."

"Someone's down here!" Mike yells. Footsteps echo.

We try to run, but I am too slow. The footsteps gain on us.

"It's Ryan!" Mike screams. He's close enough to make me out in the flashing of the headlights.

In front of us is a crappy old van advertising some car repair business. Its windows are blown out.

"Stop," I say.

I reach in the broken back window and open the rear doors. The van's floor is crammed full of car parts, including a car battery and screwdriver.

"Make for the wall," I say, stumbling to the side of the van.

I lay the car battery under the gas tank, then place the screwdriver across the terminals and pray the thing isn't completely dead.

I scramble for the wall, ankle be damned.

The battery explodes, launching the van a foot in the air and shooting flames out from under it. The gas tank catches, and there's another explosion that knocks me into a sedan. I hear shouts, and a bunch of car alarms start to blare. I make it to the wall and find Kris.

"What the hell did you find in that van?" he asks, face lit by the fire.

"Car battery," I say. "My grandfather tested old ones by touching the terminals with a screwdriver. Lost two fingers when one exploded."

"So you knew it would do that? Weren't those your friends?"

"A couple parked cars were between them and the van," I say. "And no, not anymore."

We find a door to a fire stairwell, and go up a flight.

Kris stops on the first-floor landing. "Postal people will be looking for us on two."

I pull myself up using the handrail. Goldman and his two guys can't be everywhere on the first floor.

"JCPenney should be over there," I say, opening the door on the right.

Kris turns on his light and shoves his shoulder under mine. "And we're off."

GINGER

IN THE SERVICE HALLS,
HEADED TOWARD HARRY'S (THE MED CENTER)

A couple years ago, Maddie dragged me to a corn maze—at night. She knew all about my fear of the dark, and had insisted there'd be lights and stuff plus moonlight. Naturally, that night there was no moon. And the lights—if you can call strings of orange Christmas lights, strobes, and fake torches "lighting"—were on the *outside* of the maze. But we were already inside it before I realized we had stumbled into veritable darkness.

Between the narrow paths, the death metal music yowling from the parking lot, and the sounds of torture and witches cackling, I was totally flipping out. Then arms reached out of the corn and grabbed my shoulder. I collapsed on the ground and started shrieking to be let out. The kid who'd grabbed me stepped out of his hiding place in the corn, hauled me onto his shoulder, and carried me back to the entrance. Outside, I hid behind a bale of hay so Maddie's mom wouldn't see me, then waited, mortified and freezing in my skimpy cat costume, for Maddie, who came bounding out after about a half hour.

"You beat me?" she asked, bewildered, when I popped out in front of her.

"I guess."

"Wasn't it just the best thing ever?" she asked.

I told her it had been awesome.

Now, as we make our creeping progress down the service halls, I am again faking things for my best friend. The main difference being that back then my biggest concern was that my blubbering might ruin her night. Here, if I break down, it could get us both killed. But without a face mask, Maddie cannot breathe. So our plan is to head down to the med center on the first floor to find one.

I hold tight to her sleeve and we move in sync through the suffocating blackness.

"This looks like a stairwell," Maddie whispers, holding up her glow stick to a sign on a door.

She shuffles silently through. I slide my feet forward. We get to the top of the stairs, then the door slams behind us. A lighter pops and reveals a guy's face.

"Boo!" he says, grinning.

"There's a toll for using our stairwell," a girl's voice coos below us.

Maddie rushes forward. The fabric of her cloak slips through my fingers, and I nearly topple over the edge of the first step. I'm alone.

Oh god.

No time for panic. Must breathe. I find the railing and race down.

"They're moving!" Lighter Guy shouts.

I do not stop. On the first landing, I skid around the corner and keep going down.

"They're here!" the girl's voice says from behind me.

A hand grabs my hood, choking me.

I fling my left elbow back and hit something. I'm free. I run, stumble, skip, scrabble down the stairs and land on a body.

"Ging!"

It's Maddie. She tumbles forward. I collapse on top of her.

"Move," she grunts, crawling out from under me.

I feel along the cement until I hit wall.

"I've got an exit," she whispers.

I move toward her voice, feel skin. She grabs my wrist, and pulls me through the dark until my hand touches a metal door.

"Going somewhere?"

A flame pops from a second lighter, picking out a girl's face not more than four feet from us.

Maddie points a small spray can at her. "Yes, we are," she says.

Silly string shoots from the can, hits the flame, and bursts into a fireball in the girl's face.

She screams. The fire disappears.

The metal door moves behind my back. Maddie yanks my arm, pulling me through and out of the stairwell.

"Knew that can would come in handy," she says after the door clicks shut behind me. "Grabbed it at the Halloween place."

Her breathing sounds funny.

"Use your inhaler," I say.

Two new glow sticks crack to life, lighting Maddie's shaking head. "You've seen a real attack," she says, handing one to me. "Better save it for when I'm truly sucking wind."

How long until then, Mad? What if they come after us—right now, could you run?

"Let's just get to the med center," I say instead, then put my hand on the wall and start walking.

The hall is short and leads us into the courtyard. It's eerie to see so much of the mall stretching into what seems like infinite blackness punctuated now by several spots of bright orange: more fires.

"Harry's is back this way," Maddie says. Her voice is hushed. She must have noticed the fires.

Harry's security gate is half open. We feel around and find the makeup counter that served as the check-in point for the sick. I prick my finger on something. Sneaking my glow stick out from my sleeve, I see that the glass top of the counter has been shattered.

Farther in, the curtain partitions have been knocked over. People have ransacked this place. People might still be ransacking this place . . .

Someone coughs near enough to where I'm standing that I startle and hit a curtain, which knocks something else and sends it clattering to the ground.

"Is someone there?" A guy's voice, the cougher. "Please, if you're there, come here and help me out of this gurney." He coughs again. No way I'm going in there. "Security tied this plastic cuff to my wrist and I can't get off the stupid bed. Please, just help me get off of here." Security must have tied the sick down to keep them from escaping—I'm suddenly glad I was only put in jail.

Maddie waves her glow stick side to side at me: our symbol for "No."

We shuffle on. He keeps begging.

"Please! I need a drink! Water! Anything!" *Cough.* "Please, don't leave me!"

Tears well up. I'm a coward. A stupid, weak, horrible coward. This guy is going to die and it's my fault.

"We should help him," I squeak.

"We only help each other," Maddie replies, turning around. "We did not tie him to that bed." She holds both sides of my face, her glow stick lighting our skin a freakish pink. "This is not on either of us."

I can tell that he has gotten to her too. Her eyes are shiny.

I nod, take a step, and trip. Over someone. A person. An adult.

"Maddie!"

This woman is not dead from the flu. There's a hole in her forehead.

"MADDIE!"

"Shut up!" Maddie hisses.

We kneel in front of the woman. Maddie begins to pat her down.

"What are you doing?" I manage. My voice is a trickle of sound. I'm barely able to muster the air to speak.

"Win," Maddie says. She flicks on a flashlight. "Look what she had in her pocket."

It's a tiny flashlight, one of those little metal ones, but

who cares? Its light is brilliant in the black. I lunge over the body to get closer to it.

"Chill," Maddie says, passing it to me.

I hold it up to Maddie's face, then back to mine, shine it over the whole room, desperate to see again, to really *see*.

I regret that decision immediately. There's another body with a gunshot to the head. Around the gunshot victims are other bodies, on gurneys, on cots, just slumped on the ground. Dead kids, dead adults. Flu victims. This place is no longer a med center. It's a morgue.

I kneel beside the body I tripped over. She had a flashlight; she might have masks or some medicine, something useful so we can just leave, right now.

"I already checked her pockets," Maddie says, blinding me with a beam of light. She's found a second flashlight on the other gunshot victim.

"What if you missed something?" I retort. "See, here's a pen."

"Fab," Maddie says. "You can write me a prescription for an inhaler."

"How 'bout a get-out-of-quarantine-free note?"

"*Dear Government People, The air is toxic, so I had to leave the quarantine. Sorry if I spread the deadly flu. Kisses.*" Maddie blows one into the air.

We try to laugh, but then Mad starts wheezing and I have to dig out a bottle of water to help her get it under control.

I sit back on my heels. "Maybe the supplies are in the back?"

Maddie nods.

The fabric walls are undisturbed near the stockroom doors. People cough in the dark beyond them, some crying, some calling for help. We ignore them.

In the stockroom, we find what we came for. There are boxes of particle masks. We stuff our bags and pockets. I slip two masks over my face, then sling five more around my neck.

"We should sleep in here," Maddie says.

"No." The word escapes my lips without my having even thought about it.

Maddie flashes her light at me. "This is the safest place we've found."

"We have different ideas about safe," I say, thinking of the bodies, of the dying, outside the stockroom door.

"We don't have to worry about the dead, and security chained everyone else in here to their cots." She's flipping her fingers up one by one, counting off reasons like reason has any credibility in this place. "Plus, none of the crazies from outside are coming in here—I mean, if they haven't made it past that gore-fest by now, they're not coming. There is nowhere else in the mall with these kinds of built-in security measures."

"It smells."

She can't argue with that. The bodies are starting to rot, and the stench fills the whole store.

Maddie's light shrugs. "I'd rather gag on some corpse stink than be woken by some random person ripping my bag from my body."

She doesn't say it, but the words *rip* and *body* make me

think of all the other things people could do to me in the dark. I'd never even see them coming.

"Okay," I mutter.

We find a corner and sit shoulder to shoulder. We place our glow sticks in front of us on the floor. I stare at them as if they are the dying embers of a fire. I think of marshmallows. Maddie is somehow able to fall asleep. I feel her breathing gently on my shoulder. I watch the glow sticks fade, knowing that even if I shake them brighter, they will only grow dim again.

Maddie's coughing jostles me awake. She is folded over her bent knees, hacking and wheezing. Each inhale is a quick suck of air, like she's drowning, and each exhale a slow whine.

I snap on my flashlight and begin pawing through her bag. Every tube I pull out is a glow stick—where's the goddamned inhaler?

I dump the bag. Stuff rolls everywhere. I pounce on the inhaler and pass it to Maddie.

She takes a single pull.

"Maybe we shouldn't have slept in a dusty stockroom," she manages between gasps of air.

The air is thick and still, and the corpse smell has increased by, like, a billion. Even through my mask, these things are obvious.

"We should get out of here," I say.

"Moving makes it worse," she whispers. "Just give me a minute."

"Shouldn't you hit the inhaler again?"

"It's nearly empty."

Meaning she isn't sure this will be the last attack, or the worst. She's saving her breaths.

"I'm going to look for drugs," I say.

"I'm not sure now is the time to experiment with getting high, dearest." Maddie takes a sip of water, closes her eyes.

"Inhalers," I say, trying to gather the contents of her bag from the shadows. "They have to have medication in here for regular diseases, right? I mean, they took down people's illnesses that first night. It must have been for a reason."

Maddie shrugs. "I just can't believe I wasted puffs those nights we tried to get into the parties." She holds up the measly little life-saving cylinder. "I never even got to dance."

"Choking to death and you're still thinking about parties," I say.

"Focus on the good stuff, right?"

Harry's has two floors. If it were up to me, I'd keep the drugs in the second-floor stockroom, which is the place farthest from the only accessible entrance. I leave my bag and Grim Reaper cloak with Maddie and head out, picking my way across the first floor to the escalators.

There are no curtains on the second floor, so my flashlight illuminates the whole place. It's just bodies on cots. Row after row after row. Dead bodies. Like a cemetery without the dirt. Then one coughs. I have to keep going.

One foot in front of the other, I shuffle between the cots, flashlight beam scanning the faces to see if any are alive enough to attack me. After the first few, I shine my beam elsewhere. I knock into a cot and a bloated arm flops against my leg. I keep walking. Groans in the dark. Screams from the mall outside. I keep walking.

The stockroom door is open. Blocked by a body. Another gunshot victim. Why would anyone go on a shooting spree in this place? Like there wasn't enough dying going on in here? What is wrong with people? And for a moment, I forget why I came here and am simply overwhelmed by the need to run. Run anywhere. Go anywhere else.

But there is nowhere else to go. I pinch my skin until I can control my breathing. I wipe away my tears with a sleeve. I have to focus.

Around the body, on the floor, are plastic bags and tubing, as if someone were tossing supplies like confetti.

Supplies.

My flashlight catches a stack of plastic boxes—one has a snarl of tubing sticking out. The first is full of catheter bags. Gross. The next has masks, the one after, gloves. And then, buried under all this useless stuff is a box marked TAMIFLU.

I have heard of Tamiflu. There was something on the news, back when I had news, about the terrifying shortages of Tamiflu should there be a pandemic.

What the hell is flu medicine doing hidden under all this other crap?

The doctors were saving it. For what? Themselves? Fat lot of good that did them. Well, they can certainly spare some. I grab two doses—there's only me and Maddie.

Sweeping my light, I find a table covered in papers and doctor stuff, some pills, but no inhaler pumps. Then beds—not many. Maybe these were the special patients?

Special how?

I see two little girls—and Marco's girlfriend. Ex-girlfriend? Who cares? I haven't seen her since things were normal . . . I mean, more normal than this—but whatever, she hugged Marco. Lexi was so jealous, Maddie and I tried to comfort her by telling her about that complete jerk Kevin Reamer.

God, Kevin Reamer. How awesome would it be if the only thing I had to worry about was whether Kevin still liked me?

Focus! Okay, so Marco's ex-girlfriend, two little girls—these three are alive-ish. I see them breathing, but they aren't moving, and the ex-girlfriend doesn't wake up even when I pinch her (through the sheet, of course).

There are other beds, but I'm done exploring. Sick people in beds have nothing to do with Maddie and our immediate problem. Back to the table: useless paper, useless pills. I check the shelves behind it: nothing, nothing.

I scan the rest of the wall. *There.* A cabinet. It's been ransacked, of course. Knocked-over bottles, pill packets scattered like cards, a puddle of sticky, cough-syrupy-smelling goo. I rummage through the mess. Toward the back of the bottom shelf, mixed in with some tampons, I strike gold. One inhaler pump. *Hallelujah!*

I grab the purse hanging on the side of the ex-girlfriend's bed and jam in the inhaler pump, a big bottle of Tylenol, some antibiotics, and the tampons. The Tamiflu I leave in the pocket of my jeans. I slip the strap over my chest and head back out into the field of death.

■   ■   ■

"Look what I found!" I say, waving the pump over my head as I return to our stockroom on the first floor.

Maddie shines her flashlight at me. "Just the one?"

"At least we have one," I say, forcing a smile. "That should last you—"

"Is it full?" she interrupts. Her voice is part wheeze. "Doesn't matter." She takes several long pulls from her inhaler. "If we have a spare, then I'm living large while I can."

"Don't waste that one." There was only the one tube, Maddie!

"This isn't wasting, it's using." She takes a final pull. "With the air as crappy as it is, I'm going to suck them both dry in a day."

"Even with the mask?" I say. "Even if you wore two masks?"

Maddie shrugs.

This line of questioning is making me depressed. New subject. "So where should we start looking for Lexi?" I ask, pulling my cassock over my head.

"Somewhere outside this morgue." Maddie picks up her bag.

It hits me. "The senator," I say.

" . . . is a bitch?" Maddie finishes.

"No," I say. "I mean, yes, but she evacuated everyone who wasn't sick, right? So the only drugs left in here are flu drugs, meaning maybe all the regular drugs are—"

"In the HomeMart?" Maddie adds, her eyes widening.

"Yes!" I squeal.

"Holy crap," Maddie says. "So we just have to break open the sealed security gates, knock out all of what remains of the stun-gun-wielding security brigade, and ask nicely if we might have some life-saving medicine from the woman who locked us out here to die."

"Har, har," I say. "No, we find Lexi and *then* knock on the door and get the senator to let us in like she promised. Just because that idiot security guard didn't know about her deal with us doesn't mean that she wouldn't honor it if we showed up with Lexi."

Maddie sighed. "So we just have to pray we find Lexi in this giant mall in the dark while avoiding being killed or worse by our fellow mallmates before I choke to death."

"Marco!" I say, finally feeling in control. "Like you said before, he knows something about Lexi. And I just saw his girlfriend up in the stockroom. We trade that info for info on Lex."

Maddie considers my plan, then shrugs. "I have to admire your confidence."

"Let's admire while we walk."

The plan will work. My plans always work.

R Y A N

INSIDE THE JCPenney

When we finally reach the JCPenney, all we find is a maze of discarded racks and piles of clothing. Then we run across the first group of kids. They're lying in the dark, some on cots, others on the floor, hugging. When they see Kris's light, they cower.

"We've got nothing! No food!" one says, throwing up his hands.

"The Reign of Goldman?" Kris asks as we walk away.

I nod. "His plan was to hustle kids for food."

We head out into the main part of the store. Dim light from the first-floor courtyard gives the place a spooky glow. As we search under cots and in piles of bedding, Kris and I whisper Shay's and Preeti's names, hoping they might come to us.

The main areas are abandoned. I guess they're too

exposed. But there are more stockrooms to search. In them, we find other terrified kids, but no Shay. After the second one, I tell Kris to go in alone. He can search faster without me hanging off his arm.

I keep thinking I hear something.

"Goldman?" I recognize the voice as one of the security guys. "Hank, you in here?"

I flatten myself against the wall.

The security guy comes in through the main entrance, waves his flashlight around, and catches Goldman not twenty yards from me.

"Christ, Marshall!" he yells.

I drop to the floor and army-crawl away from the wall.

"I saw you, Ryan Murphy!" he shouts.

There's a deep shadow in front of me. Must be some kind of hallway.

"Tina was a good woman!" he shouts. He kicks garbage, scrapes a cot along the floor tiles to make it clear he doesn't give a crap if I know where he is. "Not that an animal like you cares."

I drag my body slowly across the floor, trying not to disturb even the dust bunnies.

"What I want to know is how you did it," he continues. "I'm guessing you got her stun stick from her? Zapped her with that, then knocked her dead?"

My hand hits wall. I pull myself up it, then shuffle deeper into the black.

Fingers slap across my mouth.

I bite at the flesh. I'm not going down easy.

"It's me!" Kris whispers into my ear. "I heard him and figured you'd make for this shadow."

Goldman doesn't have Kris's instincts. He's heading in the opposite direction.

"He only wants me," I say. "You go, find Shay."

"Don't be such a drama queen." He shoves me. "Keep walking. The bathrooms are down here. We'll hide in there."

I shuffle silently into the dark until my fingers find a door frame. I push open the door and we end up in what Kris's light reveals to be a lounge.

"Ladies' room," he says.

We keep going, into the regular bathroom.

"Help." Someone's in one of the stalls.

Kris's light swivels around. "Stall two," he says.

I stand to the side, then silently sweep the door open. I know this girl.

"Preeti," Kris says, and falls to his knees in front of her.

It's obvious she has the flu. She's lying on the floor of a toilet stall, her forehead is hot, and she's coughing blood.

I check the other stalls. There's no one else. But Shay came here looking for Preeti. She would have found her in the bathroom. Unless—

"Did Shay find you?" I ask.

Preeti doesn't answer.

Shay can't be dead.

"We have to get her out of here," Kris says, mopping Preeti's brow with a strip torn from his shirt.

If Preeti's alone in here, Shay must be dead.

The door into the lounge squeals open. Kris shuts off his light.

"Got you now, Murphy."

It doesn't seem to matter if Goldman takes me or not. I go to stand, but Kris pushes Preeti into my chest.

"Save her," Kris whispers, "for Shay."

The door into the bathroom squeals open. Before I can say anything, Kris turns on his book light and flashes the mirrors. Blinding light bounces everywhere.

Goldman yelps, throws an arm up to cover his face. Kris shoves him in the chest, pushing him through the doorway, and runs out of the bathroom. After that bright light, the dark is full of washed-out trails, like burn-in on a TV. I hold my hand over Preeti's mouth.

"You little asshole!" Goldman shouts. Doors open and close. Footsteps slap the tiles in the hall.

He'll kill Kris. Even once Goldman sees he's not me, he'll still do it. I have to get out there, stop him.

Preeti groans.

If I do that, I waste what Kris gave me: A chance. I can't piss on a gift like that. But Preeti and I have to leave this bathroom. The second Goldman catches Kris and realizes his mistake, he'll be back for me.

There's no way I can carry Preeti and walk. But I could drag her. I crawl through the dark to the door, then find the couch I remember seeing in the lounge. There was a torchiere lamp next to it. I grab the lamp and a seat cushion and haul both back to the bathroom.

I feel my way across the tiles to Preeti, then snap the top and the base off the lamp, and rip the cord from the tube. I wrap Preeti's chest to the cushion with it, then tie the ends and sling the loop across my chest. Using the lamp's tube as a crutch, I drag both Preeti and myself out of the bathroom, through the lounge, and out into the store.

Kris's light bounces across the courtyard, toward the med center. I lean one arm against the wall of the entrance, shift the cord to pinch a different rib, and drag her toward the bottom of the nearest escalator. Just as I am about to step onto it, a light flashes on at its top. I sink into the deep shadow on the outside of the handrail.

"Halt, security asshole!" It's Marco.

All around the second-floor railing, headlamps shine down. They focus on Kris and Goldman. Kris's light goes out.

"What is this?" Goldman says, hand shielding his eyes. He's standing near a potted tree. The headlamps move like laser sights over his body.

"Oh my god, it's you!" Marco shouts. "Hey guys, it's Hank Goldman, head of security!"

Voices whoop and cheer.

"Marshall! Kearns!" Goldman calls.

"It's even better that it's you," Marco continues. "Not only do we get retribution for the attack in the pet store, but I personally get to thank you for that lovely time you electrocuted my balls."

"Who the hell are you?"

An arrow appears in Goldman's chest. He cries for the other two guys again and falls to his knees.

"Señors Kearns and Marshall, come on out!" Marco sounds like he's running a goddamned game show.

The headlamps flash around, searching the first floor. Other voices repeat Marco's call, twisting the words into a chant.

I hold Preeti tight. We are under the lip of the second-floor hallway, hidden by the bulk of the escalator. No way their lights can find us.

The headlamps move on. Their voices echo from the opposite end of the mall. I lug Preeti across the courtyard, making for the dim shadow of the potted tree I saw next to Goldman.

I find Kris searching his pockets. Goldman's dead.

"This guy is a gold mine," Kris says, then laughs. "Gold-man, gold-mine. *That's* humor."

"You seem happy for a guy who just almost got killed."

"The key word there is *almost*." Kris pulls the Taser from Goldman's belt. "I'm not dead yet!" he says in this weird accent. "Monty Python?"

I shrug.

"Kids these days," he says. "Undo that cord before you're cut in half."

We both fight with the knot I made using the plug.

"You're getting in the way," he says, slapping my hand. He gets a nail in the loop and loosens the wire.

"Thanks," I say.

"Costuming elementary school musicals," Kris says, "you get good at untying knots."

"For saving my life, you ass."

"It wasn't only your life I was saving," he says.

The plug snaps and Kris catches Preeti and her cushion. Her breathing seems worse for having been dragged around.

"She needs water, medicine," Kris says.

"The med center?"

Kris hefts her into his arms, and we make for the old Harry's.

DAY
SIXTEEN

THE
SENATOR

AUDIO LOG

Day sixteen. This is my second daily audio report. Again, delivered to a machine. I assume this was your intention from the start, perhaps on the advice of counsel?

The temperature in the HomeMart has risen to a stifling eighty degrees. Please investigate if there is some way to run the ventilation system from outside the mall. I am concerned that this stale air will only lead to a more rapid spread of the contagion. Not to be alarmist, but I also think I smell smoke.

The rationing completed by security has resulted in our having food for at least three days. That was yesterday. Please call me back to let me know if you have a plan in place concerning bringing in additional food.

A young boy was found ill last night. Security removed

him from the facility to the great distress of his mother. When offered the choice of remaining in the HomeMart or leaving with her child, she left.

My child and husband are out there in the mall. I have to assume at this point that Arthur is dead. His prognosis was not good before the power failed. Lying alone in the dark for days cannot have improved anything.

But Lexi, my daughter. She could still be out there. And I am in here. I do not like what it says about me that I am more scared of going out there and finding her dead than staying in here and waiting for you to kill us all.

As previously requested, please do call me back if you're going ahead with that plan. It's common courtesy to inform people before you blow them up. We dropped leaflets on Japan before the bomb.

SHAY

INSIDE HARRY'S (THE MED CENTER)

There's something unnerving about waking in the dark. All the more so when you have no idea where you are, and water is dripping on your face.

Last thing I remember, I had the flu, was coughing blood and running to the med center in the old Harry's department store with Preeti's two friends. Taking them with me was the only way I could convince Preeti to leave me and go to the HomeMart—I would save her friends if she saved herself.

"Hello?"

No answer.

I'm in a bed? Yes. This is definitely a sheet and blanket, and I'm sitting on a mattress and yes, this wet thing feels like a pillow. Why are the lights out? And where is the water coming from?

"Is this the med center?"

I am answered by a groan—not a human noise, but some structural sound from the building. The building sounds broken. I don't remember the building being broken.

Wait. I don't feel sick. I'm alive! I survived this flu! But why do my eyes burn?

Contacts. I slept with my contacts. I use the old sleepover trick of bathing the lenses in saliva, then slipping them back in. On the disgusting side, but effective enough.

Not that this helps—there are still no lights. What happened to the lights?

"Help!"

The building moans again and then there's a snap and a flash of spark. Something is very wrong.

But I am alive. Preeti is safe.

There's a penlight in my bag, which has gone missing. I feel down the side of the bed for it and my hand is tugged back. There's something attached to my skin. A needle digs in when my wrist bends. An IV. Totally normal, hospital stuff. *Breathe.* I follow the tube from my arm up to an empty plastic bag.

So I *am* in the med center. And I've been here long enough to drain an IV bag.

It's actually more unnerving that this pitch-black, silent-but-for-the-groaning-building room is in fact the med center. Things were bad when I got sick; apparently, they have gotten worse.

Ryan.

I have to get out of here. I have to find him.

The IV needle slides easily from my skin. The bag containing my extremely necessary penlight is not beside the bed on the floor, it's not on top of the sheets, it's not under them. But there is something poking my leg. Not my bag, but a notebook and laptop.

The light from the computer's login screen is like a beacon. I can make out the whole room—though it's just different depths of shadow. It's a stockroom. There are other beds—beds with bodies in them. Not one of the bodies moves, though, nor did any answer when I called.

I'm in a morgue.

No. It can't be. In front of me is a table. It's messy with papers and pill bottles, IV bags filled with fluid. A stethoscope. Doctor things for living patients. There's one chair. A mug. Is that shiny thing a food wrapper?

I dive out of bed. There's some liquid in the cup. Black coffee? I'm so thirsty, I don't care. There are crumbs in the wrapper. They are delicious.

The computer lies open on my bed, tilted back in the sheets. Its light shows the trickle from the ceiling. There's a crack in the concrete.

Two other beds are lined up next to mine. I think the girls in them are Preeti's friends. I wait, watching. Yes, the sheet moved. They are alive. This is definitely not a morgue.

The building groans again. The drip that had been falling onto my pillow is now a steady stream, glittering in the dim light.

Where is this water coming from?

My bag is not hanging anywhere near my bed. I sweep the floor with the computer screen and find a dead guy. He's slumped against the footboard of my gurney. But he's not dead from the flu. This guy's been shot.

It's Dr. Chen—the man in the hazmat suit that I pulled from the rubble after the riots, when we were first locked in. He was there when I found Nani. And now he's been shot.

Security wouldn't shoot the doctors, would they? I mean, Ryan said they were out of control, but *that* out of control?

Mike has a gun. And he's crazy enough to shoot people. But if Mike is shooting doctors, it means the whole mall society—security, rules, everything—is gone. There's nothing holding Mike or anyone else back.

Breathe.

The login on the computer screen is automatically filled in as "SChen." This is Dr. Chen's computer. I check the notebook; it's also his.

Did he leave me a note? Is that why this was in my bed?

Most of the notebook is all incomprehensible doctor babble. I skip to the end, where I guess he would have left his note to me. On the last page, *Tamiflu?* is circled. Then there's this: *Evidence suggests mutation Stonecliff 2 is far less virulent. Appears vaccine effective at producing relevant antibodies. Hypothesize standard antivirals may also prove effective at decreasing mortality rates. Continuation of quarantine unnecessary—no risk of pandemic from Stonecliff 2.*

I have to steady myself against the wall. Is this what I think it is? Yes. It's right there. *Quarantine unnecessary.* They can let us out. This can all be over.

Then why are we still here?

The government doesn't know. I bet even the senator

doesn't know. Of course they don't know. We'd be out of here if they knew.

I have to tell them.

I sit the laptop in a dry corner of my bed and shake the girl closest to me—Sahra, I think.

"Wake up!" I yell.

We will get out of here. We will run to the HomeMart and bang on the door until they let us in. I'll show them the notebook. We can get out of here. All of us—Preeti, the girls, me, Ryan. This nightmare can end!

Sahra rolls her head on the pillow, grumbles something about hating grilled peppers, and falls back asleep.

I shake her again. She must wake up. The stream of water from the crack in the ceiling has become a veritable waterfall.

Oh no.

The ice skating rink is above Harry's. If there's no power, there's nothing to keep the rink frozen . . .

Something crashes outside the stockroom. It could just be the building, maybe the ceiling cracking some more.

"Dammit!" a voice yells.

Not the building.

This notebook has to get to the HomeMart. It's the only thing that matters.

If I head straight between the rows of beds back there, I'll hit a door that must lead into the service halls. It takes a few tugs, but I pull the IV pole off the gurney and tuck it into my waistband across my back—it's no gun, but it'll have to do. I close the laptop, drowning the room in darkness, and shove it and the notebook into a computer bag I found on the table, then start walking.

Preeti's friends will be fine. No one bothered me while I slept; no one will bother them. The ceiling will hold.

I feel the first bed. It should only be twenty more steps or so to the door. More beds, more bodies.

My fingers brush the door, which opens into more darkness. I find the wall, and keep going down the service passage. The floor is, for the most part, clear, littered in places with what feels like paper, then my foot hits something solid.

A hand clasps my thigh. "Help me," a voice wheezes.

I could stop, help this one man, a man who's done nothing wrong, isn't even hurting me. I could help him back into the med center, find him a bed, get him water.

"Please," he says, and pulls on my bag.

"I'm sorry," I say, tugging his fingers from the strap. "Please let go."

"Don't leave me," he cries, gripping harder.

I pull out the IV pole and smack. The hand goes away.

Helping one person helps no one.

I keep the IV pole in one hand, place the other on the wall, and keep walking.

GINGER

Y ou know that black sweater?" Maddie asks.

We've stopped on our way to interrogate Marco to give Maddie a chance to catch her breath. It's concerning because we're still on the first floor, only half-way across the courtyard in front of Harry's.

"You are not allowed to start giving away possessions," I say, nipping that morbid conversation in the bud.

"Like I'd give that one away," she says, then takes a pull on her inhaler. "I want to be buried in it. Or at least *with* it."

"Even in death, you remain jealous of how amazing I looked at Jake's party?"

"I'm just saying." She takes a sip of water. "If I catch you in the sweater, my ghost is totally haunting your skinny butt."

I want to say, *Please, promise?* But Maddie's not going to die, so it's a moot point.

"We need to keep going," I say, glimpsing her face mask

under the flashlight. Its outer surface is coated in a fine mist of black, and soot sparkles in the beam. "The air has gone from bad to glittery."

"Only in this place is glittery worse than bad." Maddie refits her mask over her face.

"Put on two," I say, handing her a mask from my hoard, and she does.

The escalators have not been claimed by lunatic toll-takers, thank *god,* but Maddie and I climb up them as fast as possible all the same. The bowling alley looks abandoned. If a whole gang of headlamp kids were inside, wouldn't there be guards or something?

"Did that book light asshole lie to us?" Maddie whispers.

"Maybe they're in the back?"

I walk ahead, pulling Maddie by the sleeve. Off to the side of the main bowling area is a hallway with the bathrooms and offices and stuff. If I were running a gang, I would set up camp somewhere down that easily defendable hallway.

My instincts are confirmed. The instant we step into the hallway, we are grabbed.

"Get off me!" Maddie yells. I hear clothing rustle, then something (Maddie?) kicks me in the leg.

"We're here to see Marco!" I shout, hoping this serves as a kind of password. Someone—a very strong someone—is wrestling my arms behind my back.

The attackers say nothing. One person wrenches my arms while another hoists my legs so I am dangling like a human hammock. I kick, wriggle, bite, and scream until some wad of cloth is shoved into my mouth.

From the grimy taste of soot, I realize it's my mask.

I'm carried down the hall through the black.

A door opens and light blooms. It's like we've crawled out of a cave into a summer afternoon.

"Where the hell did you get all this light?" Maddie wails, like they stole it from the rest of us.

"We blew the transformer." It's Marco's voice. "We planned for certain eventualities."

"You blew the transformer?" I manage. "On purpose?"

"We had our reasons."

Other voices snicker their approval. So he's converted a band of idiots to whatever insanity he's planning. Oh crap. What if Lexi's one of the idiot converts?

"Lexi!" I shout.

"Who's Lexi?" someone asks.

"She's our friend," Maddie answers. "And Marco's."

"What have you done with her?" I demand.

My eyes adjust to the brilliant light, which shines from camping lanterns spaced evenly around the floor. The smallish room is crowded with about thirty other people, some sitting, some standing, all wearing weapons of some sort. I scan every face. Lexi's is not among them.

"Why would I have done anything with Lexi?" Marco asks. He uncoils himself from where he was sitting on the floor, rising up like some enchanted snake. "She told me to leave her alone. I did."

"She wasn't with you at whatever party happened in the IMAX?" Maddie is still struggling against the huge guy who has her by the arms. He has a hockey stick strapped to his back.

"She stopped by," Marco says, scowling. "Then she left."

Which means she could be anywhere. How will we ever find her? We need to find her.

Marco glares at me. "Wait, are you saying the senator abandoned her own daughter along with the rest of us?"

"Lexi ran off," I say, suddenly becoming angry with his attitude. "The senator asked Maddie and me to help search because security had her on lockdown, what with the mall falling into the hands of crazy people. Which I'm sure *you* had nothing to do with."

"I had everything to do with it," Marco snarls. He isn't playing the sarcasm game anymore. For some reason, this scares me more than his hulking gang of thugs.

"Well, aren't you special?" Maddie says. "Congrats on bringing down society. Now let us go."

They all laugh at her. I go cold inside. People don't laugh at Maddie. Ever.

"You have to pay the piper for your freedom," Mike says. He's hunched in the corner nearest Marco.

"We know where your girlfriend, the Indian girl, is," I yell.

"Shay was never my girlfriend." Marco steps closer. "What else have you got?"

Do we hand over the location of our candy stash? I look to Maddie. She stares at me, eyes bulging, like she's trying to telepathically communicate. Is that a yes? Then she stamps her heel down hard on the foot of the guy holding her. He screams and lets go of her arms. I get the message.

I stamp on my guy's foot, except a girl's voice cries out and my arms are free. Maddie gives her captor her signature groin kick and pulls the hockey stick from his back.

I figure kicking my captor in the groin would be useless, so I throw a punch at her face. She blocks it and I end up hitting her in the boob, but she doubles over anyway and I shove my way past her toward Maddie, who's sweeping the stick back and forth, jabbing at any of the headlamps who approach.

On the next sweep, I dive past her and kick the door open. I drag her into the hall and shut the door behind us. Maddie jams the stick through the handle, locking the door closed against the frame.

We race down the dark hallway, so much darker after those few precious minutes in the light. The door slams against the hockey stick, and the wood snaps. Maddie pulls out her flashlight. Once in the mall, we run toward the movie theaters.

"Where do you girls think you can hide in our mall?" Marco shouts. His cry echoes, mixing with the slap of several feet on tile.

"Here!" Maddie yells, gasping, and grabs my sleeve.

I stumble after her down the escalator, trying to calculate in my mind where on the second floor we will be. Maddie slows down, clicks off her flashlight. We crouch on the steps. She holds her hands over her face to muffle her breaths, which come in gasps.

Please let them pass us by.

"They're on the escalator!"

We are up and racing before we hear the first foot on the stairs.

Ten feet onto the second floor, we run into a guy wearing a black robe with a bolt of glow-in-the-dark green paint across his face. "This is our floor," he says.

Maddie's sucking air. I tug her away from the green-faced guy. Several gleaming headlamps bob down the escalator. We swerve around its railing.

"Drop to the floor," I whisper.

We sink below the lip of the handrail. Maddie crawls past me, wheezing, and I follow her down the hall.

"Hey!" the green-face shouts.

"What the hell are you supposed to be?" one of the headlamps growls.

Green-face shouts for backup. Maddie and I hide our shadows behind a garbage can. She buries her face in my shoulder, her breathing now frantic. I pat her on the back like that might help.

A swarm of green-faces gathers in front of the escalators, wincing in turn as they are blinded by the sweeping beams of the headlamps crowded on the stairs. The scene would be ridiculous if they all weren't armed to the teeth.

"Where're the two girls?" A headlamp girl, maybe the one who'd been holding me.

"They ran." The green-face holds a long metal pole with a small hook on one end across his chest like a lance. "Now it's your turn. We'll give you ten seconds to clear the steps."

"What makes you think you can tell us where to go?" Mike. It's like he's trying to start something.

Another face-painted guy emerges from the black. It's the leader we saw in the Halloween shop. He flexes his fists, each of which is crowned with metal claws. "What makes you think you can question us?"

An arrow flies out of the black, piercing the clawed leader in the shoulder. He screams.

The two gangs fall on each other. It's total mayhem. Poles and bats and chains and hammers smash and clang. People scream. I swear I hear a bone snap. How can that sound be so clear?

After less than a minute, it's over. The green-faces whimper and groan in the hallway. The headlamps scurry away, lights bouncing back up to the third floor. The cries get softer, so I assume those who can't walk are being taken somewhere by those who can. It's not until Maddie holds my hand that I realize I'm trembling.

"What just happened?" she asks. She alternates words with pulls on her inhaler.

"Why would they do that?" I ask. A body lies splayed on the bottom of the steps. Less than a minute, and some-one died.

Maddie peeks around me. "Give a guy a weapon—" She takes another pull from her inhaler. "And he's gonna want to use it."

Maddie lights a blue glow stick, then sips some water. I take a drink myself, nibble on a Snickers.

"We're back at square none," Maddie says, chewing Skittles between wheezing breaths.

"Wrong. We know Lexi was at the party. We start there. We are not giving up. We will find her, we will get into the HomeMart, and we will get you your medicine."

Maddie takes a final pull from her inhaler, then tugs a fresh mask over her mouth. "I like this in-charge Ginger."

She hugs my shoulder and I start to cry, but it's dark, thank god, so she can't see me.

R Y A N

ON THE WAY TO HARRY'S (THE MED CENTER)

The lamp pole I was using as a crutch snaps, and I fall onto Kris, who's carrying Preeti.

"Sorry," I say, grabbing onto his shoulder. "I still can't stand on the ankle."

"'There's always room for one more,'" Kris says in a voice. He adjusts his hold on Preeti, and we slog ahead.

"On the plus side," he says, "I'm going to leave this mall in amazing shape. I mean, just feel these muscles flex!"

"Meanwhile, I'll probably lose my foot. Good-bye, football."

"Well, that's why we have two, right? And the football, isn't that just to get girls?"

It isn't, I start to say, but then I can't come up with anything better, so I just laugh.

It takes us forever to make it to the end of the mall where the med center is. We hobble in, and the smell causes us both to stop.

"Something died in there," I say, collapsing against the wall of the entrance. Puke sours the back of my throat.

"I'm betting more than one thing," Kris says, scanning the space with his light.

The place has been trashed. And the air will only get worse the farther we go inside. Our eyes meet.

"We don't have a lot of options," he says.

"She's safer here," I say.

Kris lays Preeti across some chairs near the entrance. "If we're lucky, people will just take her for another corpse."

Medicine will most likely be inside a cabinet, so we head in and search the piles of crap for box-like shapes. I lift a sheet of curtain-wall and find a girl.

"Help," she whispers, and tugs her arms. She's handcuffed to the cot with plastic strips.

"Security?" I ask.

She nods. Before the blackout, they were rounding people up. The healthy went to jail, the sick here.

Kris pulls a knife from his pocket. "Gift of Goldman," he says, and cuts the ties holding her.

"Water," she says. It's more of a breath than a word.

She's half dead. Kris and I glance at each other. She looks at us like she knows what we're thinking. But she doesn't grab at us. I guess she's not hoping for much. Probably assumes we're going to leave her to die.

"I'll find some," I say.

"I'll check for others," he says.

Before I go searching for a water fountain in the dark, I decide to make myself a decent crutch from the broken pole of a curtain rod. I wrap strips of canvas curtain around the top to protect my pit.

"Kris, I need light."

He flashes the area around me. I see a short hallway on a nearby wall marked BATHROOMS. There's a kidney-bean-shaped tray in the junk pile at my feet. It'll do for a cup.

"Thanks," I say. The light swings back to where Kris is searching.

It takes me a while, tripping over crap every few steps, but I find a water fountain on the wall where I guessed it'd be. On the slow walk back, my crutch catches on something that crashes to the ground.

"You okay?" The half-dead girl flashes a tiny LED light at me.

"Where'd you find that?" I ask, pulling my crutch free and lurching the last few steps. I pass her what's left of the water.

"I found my purse," she whispers after gulping a sip.

Kris returns with a red-eyed kid. "There are more back there," he says.

"I'll clear a space."

The half-dead girl, whose name is Claire, helps me move some of the junk. I drag another cot over for the kid, then hobble to the water fountain to get him a drink. When I come back, there are two more people.

Kris is breathing hard and sweating through his shirt. "I think I covered this floor," he says. "It's not pretty. And they're not all dead from the flu. Someone came through here shooting."

That could only be Mike or Goldman. I can't decide who's more likely to have shot people in a hospital.

"Find any medicine?"

Kris shakes his head.

"They kept it upstairs," Claire says. "I was here before, for a stomach problem."

Kris sighs. "I'll go check."

I dig two more cots out of the rubble and set the two other guys on them. As I go for more water, the nearest curtain wall shifts. It's another survivor.

"I have ibuprofen!" he barks. "Nurse gave it to me when it went dark." He shakes the bottle. There are lots of pills inside. "Take it," he says. "Just don't leave me!"

I need the knife to get him free, so I drag myself to the escalator Kris went up. "Kris?"

I don't see the book light.

Bracing myself on the handrail, I hop my way up to the second floor. His light's near the far wall.

"Kris!"

"I found two girls back here!" The light shifts as he turns. Something glitters off to my left.

"What was that?" I shout. Claire's light doesn't reach much farther than the first cot.

He scans the floor. It's water. There's a crack in the ceiling, and water is raining down from it.

"Isn't the skating rink above Harry's?" I ask. With no power, the whole thing would melt in what, days? Hours?

The ceiling groans, there's a boom like thunder, and the crack splits. Water gushes. A pipe dangles. A pipe with fingers. Not a pipe, an arm. Then the whole body drops through.

Kris's light swivels back toward the wall. "Get those people ready to move!" he shouts.

As I scramble down the escalator, I hear another body drop with a sickening thunk. So that's where the senator stored the dead. Thousands of bodies, about to collapse on our heads.

"We have to go!" I shout to Claire.

She finds a gurney with wheels. I roll it to where we'd cleared the floor and start helping the ones we rescued onto it. Kris comes barreling out of the dark with the two girls, one over each shoulder.

"There's more," he says, and hands me syringes labeled TAMIFLU.

"We have a transport," I say, patting the cart. "There's a guy over there with ibuprofen who's tied to a cot."

"Add a headlight," Kris says, handing me his book light, which I clip on the front of the gurney's frame between a kid's legs.

Kris goes to collect ibuprofen guy while I load the two girls onto the gurney. Kris and the guy—who can walk—return, and we roll. Kris and I push, while Claire and ibuprofen guy kick stuff out of our way.

"We make a decent team," Kris says between breaths.

Team. It's a different word to me now.

"Yeah," I say, and push harder with my one free arm.

In the entranceway, we fit Preeti onto the gurney with the others. The thing is almost too heavy for us to move. But the floor is clearer here, so ibuprofen guy, real name Joe, helps us push.

Once we get out to the courtyard, there's a new problem. On the second floor, a war seems to have broken out.

"Things get better and better," Kris says, wiping his forehead with the hem of his shirt.

"Lord and Taylor's over there," I say, nodding to our right. "There'd be cots at least."

"Too exposed," Kris says. "Who knows how many people are in there."

"A smaller store then," I say.

"The mall offices!" Kris says, clapping his hands on the gurney.

"Aren't they on the third floor?" No way we get all these people up there.

"It's the only place I know of that's separated from the service halls, from everything, really. There's one door. We can defend one door."

I wave the crutch. "I can't defend anything."

Kris pulls Goldman's Taser from his back pocket and points the handle at me. "You can with this."

I heft the thing, and feel a ton more powerful. "But how do we get up there?"

"Left!" Kris shouts.

A shadow solidifies into a person running toward us. I level the Taser at them. "Stop!"

The person lifts a pole like she's going to bash my arm. Then freezes. "Ryan?"

My blood goes cold. "Shay?"

It's too much, too good. She drops the pole and falls into me. I wrap my arms around her, and the crutch holds us both up.

I bury my face in her hair. "You're alive."

"You're here," she says, voice muffled by my shirt.

Kris pushes us apart. "My turn," he says.

Shay bursts into a smile and hugs him.

"We have Preeti," I say. "We found her for you."

She doesn't look happy. "Preeti?" she asks, her face twisted. "But Preeti's in the HomeMart."

"We found her in the JCPenney bathroom," Kris says. "She's sick."

Shay's face hardens. "They locked her out?"

"Did you try to get her into the HomeMart?" Kris asks.

"I have to see her," Shay says, pushing past us both.

She stops when she sees the crowd, then looks back at us. "Who are these people?"

"We're trying to save them," Kris says.

I take her hand. "Help us," I say, then lay out our plan.

As I talk, her hand tightens around the strap of her bag. When I finish, she looks at the gurney, then at Kris, then me.

"I can't," she says.

"What do you mean?" I ask. "Are you hurt?"

She opens the bag. "I found this," she says, and explains her own plan. "I have to get to the HomeMart. I could save the whole mall, these people included."

It's like I understand what she's saying but still can't make sense of it. "But this is your sister," I say. "And me. I just found you."

Kris steps closer. "Did you just hear that?" he says, pointing to where the battle had gone down on the second floor. "That's the whole mall now. You'll be killed before you make it to the fountain."

She looks at the gurney, steps closer. The others shift so she can see Preeti.

Shay smoothes Preeti's hair from her cheek, and Preeti's eyes blink open. "Shay?"

"I'm here," she says. Tears drip down her cheeks.

"Please," I say, standing behind her. I'm afraid to push too hard, and afraid she'll go if I don't say more.

"I'll help," she says, reaching back and taking my hand.

DAY
SEVENTEEN

THE SENATOR

AUDIO LOG

Day seventeen.

This is the third audio report. The third delivered to a machine. Are you even listening to these? I have not received a single call from you. But I did get your text: Still analyzing situation. *No one found that comforting.*

Things have gotten pretty rough in here. A couple more kids fell ill. I decided to isolate them in a back office rather than lock them and their parents out. I just couldn't do it, not with all the screams I hear echoing around out there. Sue me!

Given your failure to respond to my requests for information, I decided to share your ultimate plans with the population in the HomeMart. We have collectively decided to try to escape. I let you know this so you can't claim shock when we pierce whatever blockades you have built to keep us inside. If you shoot us as we emerge, you are doing so knowing that we are coming.

I have decided not to accompany my fellow Home-Martians—such a cute name! One of the kids came up with it. I am going to wait here, with my family. Wait for whatever you have in store for us.

On a final note, I broke protocol and made an anonymous call to my favorite local news station. Had the number memorized since my campaign days. I left a tip that the government was planning on leveling the mall with everyone still alive inside it. Perhaps that should be factored into your analysis.

S
H
A
Y

ON THE WAY TO THE MALL OFFICES

"One more flight," Ryan says as I meet him on the landing. He's smiling like this is a group date and we're about to get our first moment alone.

I nod, let him kiss my cheek as he hops ahead of the lumbering crowd. We're now one floor up and at the opposite end of the mall from where I was supposed to be. But this is Preeti. This is Ryan. These aren't just strangers begging for my help.

Joe has Preeti, and Kris carries the two girls I abandoned on his shoulders. The two other guys drag themselves along, and Claire is with the little boy, Silas. I stay back to guard our rear.

Claire helps Silas onto the escalator. As she follows, two guys lurch from the shadows and grab her.

"Give us your light!" one shouts.

I whack them both in the head, and, thankfully, they scatter.

"We are so lucky we found you," Claire says, gasping.

"I can help you with him," I say, and hook an arm around Silas.

We make it up the last flight of steps, and down the hall to the mall offices. Kris clips his book light to the frame of the drop ceiling in the central hallway. When we open the doors to the actual offices, it's clear someone has already been through. The floor of the surveillance room—who knew there were cameras all over the mall?—is coated in shattered glass and cut wires. But at least the place is empty, and the offices themselves are mostly intact.

There are even some beds in a back room. I open Dr. Chen's laptop and place it in the middle of the floor to give us light.

Kris brings Preeti in first, and I kneel next to her cot.

"You came back," she whispers.

"I had to find you," I lie.

"No, I mean from the flu," she says, somehow able to sound annoyed even though her voice is vapor thin.

"Well, so did you," I say, and quickly correct myself, "*will* you, I mean. So will you."

She coughs, then reaches into her waistband and pulls out Nana's book of Tagore's poems. "My bag got taken," she says, "but I took this out first."

It's missing its cover now and is so rumpled, it can barely be called a book. But my eyes water feeling those pages, seeing the notes written by my innocent self, the girl whose biggest problem was that her friends hadn't called. Nani's favorite poems are dog-eared from before she gave the book to me, and Nana's too, from before he died. A whole history in curled, brown paper.

"Can you hold it?" she wheezes.

"Let me get you some water," I say, and tuck the book into the bag beside Chen's notebook.

Ryan finds me sobbing over the sink.

"We have flu medicine," he says. "She'll get better."

I drop my forehead against his chest, feel his arm wrap around my shoulders. Could it really be so easy?

Kris's silhouette appears in the doorway. "Staff meeting," he says. "Back office."

Claire and Joe sit in the chairs opposite the desk. Kris drops into the swiveling seat behind it, and starts rifling through the drawers. "We've got vitamin pills in here," he says, laying everything on the desktop, "and some crayons. Computer cable. A floppy disk." He pulls out a flat black square. "God, no one's cleaned this thing out in a decade."

"Vitamin pills," Ryan says, picking up the bottle. "With that and the medicine we got, we're golden." He sounds so happy, triumphant, like he's beaten all the odds.

"We'd be golden if it weren't for the impending probability of starvation," Kris says. "Claire and Joe haven't eaten in days, nor have any of the others, I'm guessing."

"There's dog food in the pet store," Ryan offers. "Shay and me, we can go down."

We'd be on the first floor. So close. He could help me get to the HomeMart.

Ryan and Kris talk like family, skipping the unnecessary words as they hash out whether dog food is worth the risk traveling to the first floor. Not just the risk to us, but to these others, to Preeti—if we fail.

What am I thinking, abandoning my sister for this

notebook? It's just another excuse, this week's distraction. Even if I get through the HomeMart's locked gates, get the notebook to the senator, assuming she even has a way to talk to the people on the outside, what will that be worth if Preeti dies alone, in the dark, like Nani?

The pet store plan is scrapped as too risky.

"There's a chance the madeleine cookies I left in Baxter's are still there," Kris says.

Ryan volunteers us.

Claire puts a hand on my arm. "I'll watch Preeti," she says. "We're all family in here."

"Thanks," I say, still staring at Preeti's shadow in the other room.

The bookstore is just down the hall. Ryan and I will run there, race back. Claire will watch her, and Kris will, too, and when Ryan and I return, we'll have food. Preeti will get better.

But then what?

"Take the book light," Kris says, walking Ryan and me to the front.

"No need," Ryan says, pulling the Taser from his waist-band. "This thing has a flashlight." He clicks on a bright, white beam. "Tried to zap a guy and blinded him instead."

"Whatever works," Kris says. "Just come back."

We head out into the darkness, Ryan's fingers entwined with mine.

"You look pretty badass with the pole strapped to your back," he says as we move down the hall.

"Don't let the costume fool you," I say.

"Fool me?" he says. "I've seen you throw down. You're the most badass person I know."

Now he's just brown-nosing. "You're forgetting Mike."

"Mike's just an ass," he says, completely serious. "Badass is reserved for people with a code. You have to be good to be badass."

I squeeze his fingers. He might be the first and only person ever to call a five-foot-one, ninety-pound Indian girl "badass" and really mean it.

Ryan steps over an obstacle that turns out to be a person: a hand shoots out, grabs his crutch.

"Please!" a voice begs.

I whip out my pole to whack the arm, but Ryan blocks my swing. The Taser's light reveals a boy and girl, two regular kids, curled one around the other.

"I think she's sick," the guy says, holding her gaunt face up to the light.

"Here," Ryan says, and hands him a few pills, ibuprofen. "It's all I've got."

I go to check my pockets and my hand pats the messenger bag. I guess I never took it off. But inside, there's only Tagore's poems, and the notebook.

Baxter's is not as abandoned as we'd hoped. Five candles sit atop bookcases at strategic points around the store. They give off enough light for us to see the shadows of four people holed up in the coffee bar.

Ryan shifts on his crutch. "I say we sneak in, and just take them with the Taser."

"And if its battery dies?" I ask.

"I think we can take a few bookstore guards."

"Normally? Yes. With half your limbs out of action? Less sure."

The candles spawn wide swaths of flickering shadow. "What if I create a distraction?" I say. "I can burn a book with one of those candles, get them to come after me, then run out of the store. You can get into the back, grab the cookies, and head out through the service halls."

"You're serious?"

"My badass self can handle making one little distraction."

"I just never imagined you setting fire to a book."

"Let's consider these special circumstances."

He takes my hand. "We should stick together," he says, eyeing my other hand, which grips the bag with the notebook inside. "You burn the book," he continues, "then meet me here and we both sneak back, together."

How do I tell him that I can't go back? "If I wait, I'm a target," I say. "And you'll be safer peg-legging it out through the service halls."

He half smiles. "Yeah, no," he says. "You're right."

"I can hold my own against a couple of bookstore guards."

"I know you can." He leans toward me, places a palm on my cheek. "These guys won't know what hit them."

My lips find his. The kiss starts small and grows.

"See you back home," he says, not letting go of my hand.

I kiss his fingers and then crawl across the hallway.

The candle is a cup of molten wax. I pour some out onto Nana's book, keeping a few pages dry to act as a wick. *I burn this book as an offering, Nani. Watch over me. And over Ryan, Kris, and the others. Help them take care of Preeti, while I take care of them.*

R
Y
A
N

INSIDE BAXTER'S BOOKS

The food is right where Kris said it would be. I'm safer going through the service halls like Shay planned, but I grab the box and head back into the coffee bar. I want to let her go, but I can't.

I slip down the steps and duck behind a stack of magazines. There's no sign of the guards. Shay's idea worked. But the other side of the store is hidden now by a large cloud of smoke. Maybe it worked too well.

I sneak through the stacks, maintaining cover until I hit wall. The smoke isn't from the book Shay burned. A part of the rug is on fire, and the rest is catching fast. The guards smack the flames with a poster.

"Over here!" one says, and points to a patch of rug that just caught.

The one with the poster whips it toward the new

branch of the fire. Behind him, the flap of wind feeds the flames. They spread like water across the rug.

"Shay," I whisper, sneaking around the entry wall into the dark corner we'd started at.

She's already gone. For a second, I let myself pretend she's headed back to the mall offices, but I know that's not where she went. That kiss was her saying good-bye.

I step out into the hall so I can see where she started the fire. The guards have cleared out. Their shadows move up to the coffee bar, then into the kitchen I just left. The rug's catching like it's made of gasoline, out of control fast.

I tuck the box under my good arm and start back to the offices. Across the mall, a shadow darts through a patch of light shining up from the lower floors. It could be Shay. I could go after her.

But Kris is expecting this food. So are the people we promised to help. I'm not going to let them—

A headlamp flashes on near the top of an escalator catching Shay in its light.

"Hey, Mike!" I scream, taking a chance it's him. "Over here!"

Shay runs into the darkness. The headlamp follows her. Have I made things worse? And then I see Mike down the hall, lit orange by the fire that's spreading behind me.

Crap.

"I told you I'd kill you if I saw you again," Mike yells.

I spin on my crutch and hobble into the part of the bookstore that's not on fire.

"Teammates don't cut and run," he says from behind a

bookcase. He's followed me in. "What would your brother say? Leaving your team for some girl." His words compete with the roar of the fire.

"Thad wouldn't hurt people," I say, winding around a wall of shelving. The flames climb up the nearest bookcase. Smoke blows right in my face and I drop, coughing.

"Thad would do what he had to," Mike says from the other side of the bookcase. "He would take out any opponent to save a friend."

I dare rolling over the fire, then turn the corner into another row. "You don't have to do what you do," I say. "You just *like* doing it."

The bookcase beside me creaks and leans. Books rain down on my head. I scramble away from it, down the aisle, then turn up toward the coffee bar.

"I like *surviving*," Mike says, climbing over the toppled bookshelf.

"Surviving is easy," I yell, pushing a rack of magazines between us.

He grabs my good leg and I fall on my face. I flip onto my back, and he crawls over me.

"Survival isn't easy," he says. A rack of newspapers behind him catches and shoots flaming bits of paper into the air. "But it's all we have left."

"This isn't survival," I say, not even trying to block whatever's coming. "This is kicking ass for sport. It's the easiest thing in the world. Caring about someone else, trying to help them survive? That's hard."

"You let your girlfriend go out there alone," Mike says, grinning. "How's that helping her to survive?"

"Shay doesn't need any help," I say. His eyes stand out from the smeared black that coats his skin. "But you do."

And I nail him in the gut with the Taser.

It takes all my strength to get Mike up the steps and into the kitchen behind the coffee bar, dragging him behind me, his ankles pinned between my good arm and my hip so I can use the crutch. By now, the whole bookstore is on fire and the smoke is choking thick. I pull my shirt over my mouth and crawl out to get the box of cookies, then set them on Mike's chest.

The smooth tile is easier to pull him along. I get him out of the store and down the service hall before he starts to twitch.

"What the hell?" he shouts. His feet are still limp in my hands.

"Hold still, dickhead. I'm saving your life."

"You had a Taser?" he asks after I drag him a few more yards.

"Kris took it off Goldman."

"We wondered where his went."

We've come far enough to have cleared the fire.

"It doesn't have to be like this," I say, dropping his legs and grabbing my box. "You and Marco could stop being assholes and actually help people."

"It is how it is," he says. He moves his shoulders, an arm.

"See you on the outside, then," I say, hopping down the hall.

He doesn't say anything more. He doesn't come after me either.

▪   ▪   ▪

"Where's Shay?" Kris asks when I come into the offices, which now have better lighting. Little candles that turn out to be crayons are stuck to the corners of all the desk-tops.

"She left," I say, holding out the box.

He sits in a desk chair. He rests his forehead on his hands. "I hope she makes it," he says, finally.

"You okay?" I ask.

Instead of answering, he coughs blood across the desk's blotter. I lift him, lay him down on the floor.

"Maybe we shouldn't have surrounded ourselves with sick people," he says. His voice is pinched. His head's burning hot.

"We don't leave people behind," I say, unrolling the canvas from my crutch and shoving it under his head.

He coughs blood onto the rug. "Our team needs a new motto," he says.

"How about 'No dying'?" I grab his water bottle off the desk and pour a sip into his mouth.

He swallows. "You print the T-shirts," he says. "I'll make a sign." He closes his eyes.

"Kris?" I shout.

His eyelids crack open. "I'm not dead yet," he says in that stupid voice.

"I'm going to kill you."

"Counterproductive," he grunts, and falls asleep.

GINGER

IN THE THIRD-FLOOR SERVICE HALLS

We started at the IMAX and we've been working our way out, searching stockrooms, stores, even under the tables in restaurants for Lexi. I time the pace of our search to the volume of Maddie's breaths: As she wheezes louder, I search faster. When we started, I was careful—I knocked on doors, threw in a glow stick to check for potential attackers, searched methodically and tried not to make too much of a mess—now I fling open the door, flash on my light, and tear through every goddamned corner.

We've found some people, none of them Lexi. In one stockroom, we were nearly shot by a security guard hunkered down behind a wall of shelving, his voice distorted by a fireman's plastic face mask as he warned, "I will kill both of you if you come any closer."

In the back of the sports bar, we find a pile of bodies.

All flu deaths. They must have gotten sick together and died, one by one.

"What do you *(wheeze)*, think it feels like *(wheeze)*, to die?" Maddie stares at the pile, leaning against the edge of a countertop like she'd crumble without it.

"These people died of the flu," I say. "It felt like having the flu." She shouldn't be dwelling on this. We need to keep moving. I sweep the room with my light.

"Do you think it hurts?" She takes a pull on her inhaler. "I don't remember what it felt like when I had the flu."

The bodies are bloated and smelly. Blood oozes from the eyes, the mouths, the noses. The skin of the hands and faces is splotchy black. How could they not have felt that? How could their deaths have been anything other than horrific?

"It doesn't matter," I say. "Neither of us have the flu." I flash my light in the last unexplored corner. "Lexi's not here. Next stockroom."

"I'm going to die," Maddie says.

I refuse to look at her. I storm over to the door and open it. "Let's go."

"I can *(wheeze)*, feel it."

"It's just the dark," I say. "The dark is depressing."

She laughs, wheezes, coughs. "We're tripping over bodies stacked like pancakes and you say the *dark* is depressing?"

"The dark is depressing *me*," I say, though we both know the dark is nothing compared to the sound of Maddie's breathing.

Please, Lexi, be in the next stockroom. *Please . . .*

■   ■   ■

We reach the arcade, which we know is clear, and I'm about to suggest braving the fire stairway toll-takers to begin searching the second floor, when I realize Maddie is not beside me.

"Mad?" I whisper into the black.

My voice echoes around the hall. No answer.

I fumble in my bag for my light. Turn it on. To hell with any attacker, I have lost Maddie.

The light finds her some ten feet back, slumped against the wall. I run to her.

"Mad!"

She's wheezing. I grab her bag, but she stops my hands.

"It's empty," she manages between choked breaths.

"Both?"

She drops her chin to her chest, coughing and wheezing on.

No. This is too soon. Goddammit, Maddie, you used too much. Wasted what you had! We need Lexi to get into the HomeMart, and we need to get into the HomeMart to save you!

"Okay," I say. "We go to the HomeMart and bang on the door until they answer. They can leave us out here, but they have to give us an inhaler. They have to."

Maddie feebly waves a hand. "Look at the light," she whispers.

The beam from my flashlight is a solid cone of sparkles. I can taste the air on my tongue. It's like licking the inside of a chimney.

"You'll be fine once we get a new—"

She coughs, swipes a hand at my face. "Can't make it," she wheezes. "Can't walk."

I wish I could carry her. But I couldn't carry anyone on a good day, let alone when I'm exhausted and have only eaten Snickers bars and water for days. I could go there on my own—except how could she defend herself? No, we have to stay together. But she needs air.

The security guard.

He had an oxygen mask.

He doesn't need it. He would be just like the rest of us without his mask. But Maddie, she'll die without it. I could go talk to him. Reason with him. He's a policeman. Sort of. It's his duty to serve and protect. His duty to give me his mask.

"I'm going to get you an oxygen mask."

Maddie gives me the *oh-honey* look. Screw it. I hug her, drag her as best I can flush against the wall so no one will trip over her, and then run through the dark, flashlight beam bouncing, to find that stupid guard.

His was the second door down from where we started. Or was it the third? The third is silent, no guard. So the second.

I open the door, throw in a glow stick.

"I will shoot!" he barks.

"I need your help!" I yell back.

"Go away!"

"Please!" I shine the light on myself, reveal my completely unthreatening lameness to him. "I couldn't hurt you if I wanted to."

He doesn't say anything in response, which I take as a good sign.

"I need your help," I continue. "My friend is dying."

My voice chokes on the word. I force myself to keep going. "She has asthma and can't breathe this disgusting air. Please, give me your oxygen mask. She'll die without it."

"I'm not giving you crap."

"What?" Did he just say what I think he said?

"All you teens can die as far as I care. Get out before I shoot you."

"Aren't you supposed to help people?" I manage. "Isn't that your job?"

"My job, kid, was to lock all of the healthy teens up and tie down the sick in the med center to try to keep all of you from dying." I hear a click—did he just load a weapon? "But that was before you blew the electricity. Then you killed Skelton, Goldman, Kearns. Now I'm staying locked down until I get the all clear to return to the HomeMart."

"The all clear?" I click off my light. No sense in giving him a target.

"Once you all have died of the flu or have killed each other—the all clear. I knew you kids would lose it the second security pulled out. I told Goldman. He should have stayed in the HomeMart." His feet scuffle across the ground. "You still here?" He pauses. "You better get out before I make you get the hell out. I am not dying out here, not for you animals."

I drop to the ground and crawl into his room, toward where his voice had been.

"Hey," he shouts. "I said get out of here!" His voice is quieter, echoes down the hall. He's yelling into the service passage.

The door clicks shut. "You still in here?"

I try to remember the layout. His shelf was about fifteen feet from the door, on the left. My hand hits something. The shelf? I lie down in front of it, inch onto my side to make myself invisible.

His footsteps slap on the cement toward me, then I hear clothing rustle—he must have to squeeze himself between something and the shelf to get back behind it.

What am I doing here? How am I going to get the mask from him? I need a plan. I'll wait for him to fall asleep— no, Maddie needs the mask now. No waiting. No plan. I need the mask.

The shelf.

Lying on my back, I spin my body and brace my shoulders against the floor. My toe hits a solid part of the shelf. I kick hard against it with both legs.

The shelf is heavy but this is for Maddie's goddamned life, so I push harder, put every muscle I have into it, and the thing starts to tilt.

"What the hell?" the guard screams, and then I hear the thud and crash of boxes and whatever else was on the shelf. The guard groans, yells, swears, then shouts, "I will shoot you!" and clicks on a flashlight.

He's trapped, caught between the shelf and the one behind it, suspended like a fly in a web.

I climb onto the shelf, my fingers grabbing for whatever part of him I can find. I locate what I think is an arm, then grope around until my knuckles knock on something smooth—the mask.

"I will kill you!" He reaches for me and drops the light.

The floor is now visible. I grab a metal tube lying under him. And then I kneel over his writhing body, silhouetted through the shelving, and hit him with it, anywhere, everywhere, except for where the mask is.

A gun fires.

I smash his hand. He yelps with pain and the gun clatters to the ground.

Fingers reach through the shelf, scratch my legs. I hit him over and over. The shelf shifts, like he's trying to push it. I keep going. The shelf settles. His hand falls away.

I swallow, my throat is dry.

The mask.

I pull it free. Then follow the tube to the oxygen tank, which is strapped to him. My trembling hands work the release buckle, and the tank comes loose. I lift it and the tube through the shelves.

And then I'm gone, through the black, into the deeper black of the hallway, down, down the hall, into the darkness. My breath hiccups.

It doesn't matter. He doesn't matter. He should have given it to me. He didn't need it. He should have given it to me.

My shoulder slams into the door to the fire stairwell.

Wait, I ran past Maddie.

Clever Maddie. She let me run past her.

I will my hands to stop shaking. They do not obey. Still, my fingers find my flashlight. Light! Only then do I see the blood on my hands.

Doesn't matter. I wipe them on my cheap Halloween robe. Reaper. Death.

Doesn't matter.

My light finds Maddie. She's sitting where I left her, quiet and still.

"I got the mask!" I shake her. Her head lolls.

No.

I fit the mask over her face, turn the oxygen tank to the max.

"Maddie!"

I shake her again.

"MADDIE!"

SHAY

ON THE WAY TO HOMEMART

Baxter's is more than halfway to the HomeMart. I head for the nearest escalator, and am blinded by a headlamp.

"No trespassing!" a voice shouts.

"Hello, Shay." Mike's voice.

Mike was terrifying when he was on my side. I push off the railing and make for the movie theaters. A third voice yells out—Ryan's? No, he escaped through the service halls.

The headlamper follows me into the theaters—I'm not sure if it's Mike or the other one, but I'm also not sure it matters.

My book fire in Baxter's glints off the glass display cases of the refreshment stand, meaning it's more than just a book fire now. I can taste the smoke all the way over here. I have to get down a floor.

"Where're you hiding, little girl?"

It's not Mike—that's a relief. The headlamp sweeps the lobby. Damn, those things are handy. For a moment, I contemplate fighting the guy for it—I could hide, jump out at him as he passes—but it's too big a risk. If I lose, we all lose, for sure the headlamper would burn the notebook before reading it. I slink into deeper shadow, away from the main part of the mall—I think. I end up at another door, another hall. The dark has me all turned around.

Far up ahead, there's a flashlight. The light is dim, like the batteries are almost gone, but any light is better than the no light I have.

The light is beside a dead girl, whose arms cling to another dead girl, who—hold the phone, has a freaking oxygen mask? Where did she—who cares? I tug the strap holding the mask to the girl's face.

"Get off her!"

The first girl throws herself at me, knocking me over, and lands on my chest.

"Don't touch her!" she screams, grabbing my arms.

"I'm not!" I scream back, though why I think logic will hold sway is beyond me.

"She's going to be fine! She has to be fine."

Her tears drip onto my cheek. "I'm so sorry," I say.

The girl dissolves into loud sobs. She's going to get us killed.

"Please calm down."

"We should have gone straight to the HomeMart." Her voice sounds wrung out. "We should have tried for a way onto the roof."

"There's no way out," I say. "And the HomeMart shut out my ten-year-old sister. They would not have let you in, especially if your friend was sick."

Her bloodshot eyes finally register my presence. "I know you," she says, and climbs off me. "You're Marco's girlfriend."

A laugh escapes my lips, though she is clearly not making a joke. "I am *not* Marco's girlfriend."

"I saw you hug him in the cafeteria, the courtyard," she says. "My friend. She liked him. Before he became a complete asshole."

"He *was* my friend," I say. "I haven't seen him in days. Please, just let me go. I won't touch your friend."

She snickers. "You have someplace you have to be?"

"I have a notebook," I begin. Maybe I sell her on my cause, maybe I get out of this without a fight. "It belonged to the guy who ran the med center."

"The dead guy next to your bed?"

There's a double-take moment. "You saw me in the med center?"

"You were sick," she says. "I didn't think you'd make it."

Fair enough. "The notebook was in my bed. Dr. Chen stashed it there before he died."

"Before someone shot him, you mean."

"Before that," I say.

"People suck," she says.

"Not all people."

I tell her what's in the notebook, how it could save us all.

"It can't save all of us," she says, looking at her friend.

"She wouldn't want you to die here," I say. "Not when there's a chance to get out."

Tears fringe her eyelashes. "No, she wouldn't," she says.

She pulls off the Grim Reaper cassock she was wearing and crawls to her friend. She lays it over the body like a shroud, slides the mask out from underneath, then stands.

"Okay, I'll help," she says, wiping her face with her sleeve. "I'm Ginger." She hands me the mask.

"Shay," I say, and put it on.

"Let's go," she says, and walks back up the hall I had run down. "HomeMart is this way."

Already, she's helping.

At a door down the hall, she stops. "I have to get something," she says, and disappears inside. When she comes out I don't see anything new on her, though maybe it's in her purse.

"You find it?"

"Yep."

She leads me to the exit into the main part of the mall. The fire rages in Baxter's, and seems to have spread to a neighboring store. Thick clouds of smoke billow across the glass and metal struts of the ceiling. It's only a matter of time before the entire third floor is either burning or enveloped in smoke.

"So that's what did it," she says, staring at the blaze. "My friend, she had asthma."

I don't tell her I started it.

We race down the nearest escalator. On the second floor, two green faces drift toward us.

"Cut the light," I whisper.

She turns it off and we make for the wall.

"We hide here until they're gone," I say.

Something rustles, then there's a snap, and the light of a green glow stick blooms between us. "Got the right color on the first try." She looks at my bag. "You have a pen in there?"

I hand her one, and she stabs the glow stick. She squeezes some of the glowing goo from its center, then smears it on my face. The girl is proving her worth in spades.

Faces glowing, we step out into the hallway. A green-faced patrol flashes a laser pointer at us, but we just keep walking for the down escalator. Just as we pass the escalator from the third floor, headlamps flash on.

"Green-Faces! We have come for your souls!"

Not good.

"Go!" Ginger yells, and pulls an actual handgun from her bag and starts shooting.

I break into a run for the escalator, which is now clearly visible some twenty feet ahead of us. I try to wipe the glow gunk from my face, but only succeed in spreading it to my sleeves.

Headlampers are coming up the escalator.

"There's no escape!" one shouts at me.

Wheeling around, I dart down the hall toward the food court, which is lit by a bonfire. I break into a sprint, hurdling toppled chairs and tables. I hope Ginger got away before she ran out of bullets.

Just as an escalator's handrail comes into view, headlamps click on from every direction. The nearest green-faces run at them, wielding bats and metal bars. I've stumbled into a war. I pull my IV pole free, and keep running for the escalator.

A body smashes into me from the side, knocking the breath from my lungs. I manage to slide a hand under my head before I hit the tile.

"I got one!" the guy shouts, standing over me, his head-lamp in my face.

I kick him soundly in the nuts and he falls over. Panting, gasping, I get to my knees, my feet, and stumble forward.

But the headlampers are everywhere, driving the green-faces with arrows, slingshot baseballs, kayak paddles, and spray-can flamethrowers into the food court. I spin and race back toward where I left Ginger.

Explosions. My ears ring. Somehow, I'm on the ground again. The green-faces scatter. In the fires that now consume my half of the food court, I see why: The huge circle of the Ferris wheel falls toward me. The head-lampers blew up its base.

I scramble to my feet, run in the opposite direction, across the food court. The wheel crashes to the floor, sending a tremor through the tiles that knocks me flat.

Headlamps slash the air around me. There are many fewer green faces.

"That was awesome!" one headlamper shouts.

Blend in, just act normal. I stand and attempt to walk past them.

"Where the hell are you going?" A headlamper blinds me.

"Dude, isn't that Ryan's girl?"

"Mike'll want to see her."

I make a dash for the dark beyond the food court and

get three strides before lightning sizzles over my skin and I lose control of my muscles. Like Kris, the headlampers must have stolen a Taser. I fall to the floor. My head flops against my limp arm.

Hands wrench my wrists back. I'm hauled up onto someone's shoulder. I will my body to fight, but it hangs like a doll's. They are taking me back up the steps, away from the HomeMart. I want to scream, *I can save us all!* but I've lost control of everything.

MARCO

HEADED TOWARD THE POST OFFICE

We waited and we watched and we schemed and we prepared and now the war with the green-faced gringos is *ON*.

We know they have sentries every ten feet along the second floor. We know how they signal each other using flashes from laser pointers. We know that they like to overrun attackers, leaving only a skeleton crew to man their base.

Heath is leading most of our team on a full-frontal assault. The plan is to pick off the outliers, then herd the roving patrols toward where we've set up our little surprise. The Green Faces have swarmed out to defend their home. Like clockwork.

They do not expect Mike and me. They do not know they are about to get taken down.

It's what they deserve after killing Kyle on the escalator.

The Green Faces had no idea who they were dealing with. They had no idea we already controlled the entire freaking mall.

Now they will learn.

"The halls are empty," Mike says.

"Let's move."

We are so used to the dark, used to this mall, that we don't turn on flashlights anywhere outside the bowling alley. Part of it's that we know this mall like we know our own bodies, but the rest of it's the result of experience. Even in the total black of the service hallways, we know it's better to keep a hand on the wall than to turn on any sort of light and out yourself to all the vampire kids looking to scavenge the underwear off your ass.

"Ten yards," Mike whispers. He has this scary accurate ability to judge distances. He says it's from football. Wherever it's from, it's been damn useful.

We walk, feet silent, invisible. Muffled shouts and bangs from the battle in the food court thunder through the walls. We stop. I throw a tennis ball at the wall opposite, about ten feet back from where we stand.

A flashlight clicks on next to us, showing the door sentry we expected.

Mike punches him in the face.

The kid drops.

"After you," I say.

Mike kicks in the door. Light blazes from inside the post office. The Green Faces have a crapload of lanterns.

Mike finds cover behind a sorting bin. I bolt across to the opposite wall and duck behind a shelf.

"Just the two of you?" a voice calls. "We expected so much more from the terrifying headlampers."

My eyes adjust. I nod to Mike. He tips his head to the side.

We stand and step into the room in unison—me brandishing my nail gun and Mike his Glock. Five guys are positioned in front of us, including the knife-fisted douche who runs the Green Faces.

Even better, they surround what can only be called a healthy pile of food, including what looks like—praise Jesus—a tub of freeze-dried egg. Where in the hell did they find that juicy nugget?

"Feel free to simply walk away," I say. "I'll even give you ten seconds instead of the usual five."

Knife-fist grimaces. "His gun isn't even loaded," he says, cocking his head at Mike. "Get the hell out of my post office."

"So that's a no?" Great. I shoot Knife-fist in the chest, then keep shooting nails until the other two in front of me drop.

Mike drops the empty gun, then flattens the two on the right with a bat-and-hockey-stick combo that's just killer.

I tuck the nail gun into the makeshift holster I've constructed. "How'd they know you're out of ammo?" I ask.

Mike tucks the two weapons back into the bandolier he's fashioned from strips of canvas. "Lucky guess," he says. "Maybe they saw the people in the med center."

"Huh."

I examine my handiwork. One of the two on the left is dead for sure. The other is kind of crawling away. Knife-fist is up on one elbow, glaring at me like that alone is going to inflict damage.

"You are so dead," he says.

"Is that a threat?" I ask. "Mike, I think this asshole just threatened me!"

Mike jams the Glock into his waistband and hefts the keg o' dried egg. "Let's go," he growls.

"Always so serious," I say, grabbing the other food. "The rest of them won't be back for at least another ten minutes."

He shifts the bucket to his other hand and opens the door to the service passage.

At the side hall I marked earlier with a glow-in-the-dark sticker, we turn off, stopping at the exit into the main part of the mall. The food court is filled with the flaming wreckage of the Ferris wheel. Shrieks, thuds, and crashes resound, but there are far more Headlamps than Green Faces. Total domination has been achieved.

We backtrack to the main service hallway, book it for the fire stairwell, and climb back up to our fortress in the bowling alley.

"Is it always this fun?" I ask, once we're in the mechanical room behind the bowling lanes, or Command Central, as I've come to think of it.

"Is what always this fun?" Mike says, placing the egg bucket with the rest of our food stock.

"Beating the crap out of people?"

"You tell me."

"No," I say. "I mean, on the outside. Is it this fun beating the crap out of people in the real world?"

"What does it matter," he says. "We're never going to

be out there again. This is as real as our lives are going to get."

This is the kind of thing Mike says that makes me nuts. It's like he's missing my point on purpose.

"They had less food than we thought," he says.

"That egg alone will last us a week."

"Then what?" he says. "The post office was the last place we thought there would be a big stash."

"We'll find another stash," I say. "There's always another stash."

"Yeah." He sighs, which is total passive-aggressive crap. "I'll watch the front with Laila and Jake. Two whistles means they're back."

"Fine."

It's like Mike has given up, like he's ready to just throw in the towel and die. Screw that. We are the goddamned kings of this mall. If anyone's going to live, it's going to be us.

I down an oxycontin—a gift from Mike for my busted face—and start calculating new rations for my team. We have managed to eat well every day. I have done that for my crew. It's all about the protein, and we took it wherever we could. Heath had the idea to cook animals from the pet store. Laila protested at first, said no way she was eating Fido, but then she smelled it. When you're starving, you can't be choosy.

With this egg, we are set for a week or more. And with the Green Faces in critical condition, it's probably going to be an easy week. Just defense work, manning the perimeter, that kind of thing.

We'll need batteries. Maybe Mike and I will hit up the

Green Faces for some of their lights. Ha! I just got that—hit up! Hilarious.

Mike appears in the doorway.

"Dude, you have to hear this," I say. "I was just think-ing—"

"We have a guest," he says, all cagey.

"We're running a hotel now?"

"It's Shay."

Ho-ly crap.

She's alive.

"She came here?" I ask.

"Heath and Naomi bagged her in the food court."

So she's coming to beg for her freedom. Let her beg.

I find the tallest stool in the most imposing corner and perch my ass upon it. "Well, bring our guest right in."

S
H
A
Y

BOWLING ALLEY

y brain doesn't recover control of my voice until we get to the third floor. My arms and legs hold out, willfully useless, until we're inside the bowling alley. But even after I regain complete control of my body, I keep silent and limp. Better this jerk thinks I can't escape. Better he finds out only when I bust loose and make a run for it.

"We taking prisoners?"

I know that voice—it's Mike.

"Ryan's girl," the one holding me says. "Thought you'd want to talk to her."

"You thought wrong."

"You want me to let her go?"

Yes! Please!

"Might as well send her to the back," Mike says. "Marco will want to say hello. I'll take her."

The guy holding me tries to pass me like an hors d'oeuvre, but I push myself out of his arms.

"I can walk myself," I say.

A hand clamps down on my arm. "Fine by me."

I know better than to fight Mike. Even if he weren't a cold-blooded killer, he still outweighs me by a hundred pounds.

Mike leads me through the black like he has perfect night vision. He and Marco must know this whole mall that well. Not only that, but they might control the entire mall at this point.

And it hits me like a fist: They are my ticket to getting to the senator.

"Wait here," Mike says, jerking me to a stop.

Mike opens a door, pouring light into what I now see is a narrow hallway, and speaks to Marco. He sounds like the same Marco. I wonder if this is a good or a bad thing.

"Go in," Mike says, releasing me.

Marco sits on a stool near the back of a small room bright with lights. His face is bruised, but that's nothing compared to the red welt covering one entire side of his face, from his temple down to his cheek and back over his ear. The skin is black in places, and the surface of the wound looks shiny. He must be in so much pain.

"You look like you've been sick," he says.

"I have. You look like you burned off your face."

"Only half."

Behind him, surrounding the stool, is a stockpile of food that could feed every person in this mall.

"You steal all that?"

"It's a dog-eat-dog world," he says. "Mind you, we ate

the dogs, so it's really a man-eat-dog world in here."

"You're wearing my duster."

"You left it," he says. "Finders, keepers."

It's like eighty degrees in here, there's no need for the coat. So it's all show. This whole thing, it's theater.

"Please let me go," I say. I don't play it too over-the-top. No eye-batting, no pouty lips. Just your ordinary damsel in distress.

"So soon?" he says. "You haven't even told me what you and the boy wonder have been up to! Where is that jerk-off friend of yours, anyway?"

"Ryan's saving lives," I say. "You want to give me some of your food? I could drop it off for him. Might help."

"This isn't *my* food. This is *our* food. My crew's food. I can't give you any without taking it from their mouths, and after all, they're the ones who fought to get this stuff."

"Well, there's not much more to tell," I say, shrugging, smiling. "I'd best be off."

"Really," he says, sounding interested. "You have some pressing engagement I should know about? What *have* you been doing? Because I'm told you were with the green-faces. And we have a policy of extermination regarding those particular assholes."

Am I to understand that, had his friend not recognized me, Marco would have had me killed?

"I put the goo from the inside of a glow stick on my face to cross the second floor," I say.

"You always were a clever one," he says. "Now tell me where you got the glow stick."

He's smiling like this is all just a game, like the lives of every single person in this mall aren't riding on this exchange. Truth seems to be getting through to him. Let's see how the whole truth and nothing but lands.

"I can get us out of the mall," I say.

"Did Dr. Who show up with his magic police box? Or was it Captain Kirk who offered to beam you up?"

I reach into my bag.

"Not so fast," he says, sitting upright, preparing to strike, as if I'm reaching for a concealed weapon.

"It's just a notebook," I say, holding open the flap of my bag. "But it contains the last notes of Dr. S. Chen, who discovered that the mutated version of the flu is a better flu. It can't cause a pandemic. We are no longer a threat to humanity."

"Whoop-de-freakin'-doo." Marco twirls a finger above his head. "Thank you, Dr. Chen, for that little newsflash. I'm sure all the nice men with guns surrounding the mall give a rat's ass whether we're contagious."

"They don't know about what he found yet," I say. "I—*we* have to tell them. The senator has to have some way to communicate with the outside. We just need to get her these notes, and then she can call the person running things for the government. This can all be over. Once the people on the outside know we're safe, they'll let us out."

Marco snorts a laugh.

I'm not sure what he thinks is funny. I continue, "And you and Mike, you know this mall so well, you could get me there. It would take, like, five minutes." I'm not above flattery. "No one would bother me, not if I'm with you."

Marco slides off the stool, approaches. "I hate to be the first to tell you this, Shaila, though really, how you missed it is beyond me, but"—and he's in my face—"WE. ARE.

DEAD TO THEM. The people on the outside don't care if we've discovered the secret to world peace in here. They don't want to hear from us, not ever, not about anything. They have completely cut us off. There's no white flag to wave, no Oh-Crap button to push if things get really bad. Because let me tell you, if there were, the senator would have pushed it long before now.

"You think she hasn't told them anything and everything, including that we're all fine and please let us out now, over her phone or CB or soup can? Do you honestly believe that she hasn't used everything in her bullshit arsenal to try to get them to open up the doors, even just for all the nice people in the HomeMart? You think she has a shred of credibility left with the people on the outside?

"God, I see it in your face. You really thought this would work. You really thought you were going to pop your head out and everything was going to be sunshine and daisies. You thought there was a happy ending to all this.

"Well, sorry to crush your little dream of being our savior, but really, Shay. You've got to face facts. And the facts are not in your favor."

My hands begin to shake.

"I have to try," I say. "Just let me try."

"No." He walks away from me.

I run at him.

Marco mule-kicks me in the chest and I fall.

He kneels over me. "Shaila, Shaila," he says. "Tsk, tsk. No attacking from behind. It's not sportsman-like."

I gasp for breath.

The door swings open and slams against the wall.

"This girl had a gun," a guy says. He pushes Ginger in

through the door and she sprawls onto the floor beside me. "Won't say where she got it, but must have been from security."

"You are such an asshole!" she yells back at the guy in the doorway.

"Everybody's so angry," Marco says, ascending to his perch. "Why is everyone always so angry?"

Ginger cradles her hand in her lap. She's wrapped the bottom of her shirt around it. The fabric is dark with blood.

"Just let us go, Marco," she says. "This whole gang thing is ridiculous enough without you taking prisoners."

"But we're all having so much *fun*."

Ginger glares at him. "I'm not. Lexi wasn't. Or did you forget about her? All she wanted was to go on a date with you and you treated her like crap, all to join this stupid gang. And now she's disappeared, probably dead. And that's probably your fault too. If you'd thought about any-one besides yourself."

"I think about other people all the—"

Ginger stands. "If it weren't for this ridiculous gang, you might have saved her."

Marco has collapsed into a mean, dark knot. "What the hell do you know about it?"

"I know you were the last one to see her alive. I know she came to you for help."

I get to my knees beside her.

"We're not even asking for your help," I say, continuing on her thread. "Just let us go. If we die, we die. If we're crazy, we're crazy. If we fail, then you were right and we're all dead anyway, so who cares."

Marco sits back. His face brightens. "Ah, but if you succeed, then I'm wrong, and I'd hate to give you another shot at making me look like an asshole."

Everyone will not die because I broke one loser's heart. "Then keep me here," I say. "Let Ginger go."

"I'd be happy to make you look like an asshole." Ginger rips the hem of her shirt and winds it around the bleeding hand.

"Exactly," he says. "So you see why I can't let either of you go. Now, if you had something to trade, like that glow stick, or perhaps where and how the hell you got your hands on a gun?"

"How about a cure for the flu?" Ginger says.

"You have a cure for the flu?" Marco asks, eyes wide.

Something he cares about?

"It's an antiviral," she says, pulling a syringe of Tamiflu from her back pocket. "It can make the illness less serious."

Tamiflu. The notebook. Dr. Chen must have given it to me, I was his test subject.

"It *is* a cure," I add. "I had the new flu, and this stuff saved my life."

Marco holds out his hand. "Give it to me."

Oh my god, this could work. Please, let this work.

She places the tube in his palm.

"We can go?" I ask.

He walks out of the room and the door slams closed behind him.

M
A
R
C
O

STAIRWELL NEXT TO THE BOWLING ALLEY

I almost trip over my feet going down the fire stairwell. But I can't slow down. I go faster, jump flights, land at the bottom and burst out the door into the thick darkness. Fifteen paces in, I hit the fender of her car. I open the door and the dim overhead light blinks on.

Lexi.

She groans, her head rolls away from the light.

"I have something for you," I say.

I crawl into the back of the car, and dribble some of my Tylenol-Sportade concoction between her lips, just to get her in the drinking mood. Then I slip the syringe into her mouth and press the plunger.

Lex, no matter if this stuff works or not, you have to know that I'm the one who saved your life. Not your mom, not your friends—me. Marco Carvajal. Life saver.

I'm the one who found you in that stockroom, curled

under a shelf and wrapped in bubble wrap like a blanket, so still I held my cheek to your lips to make sure you were breathing.

Why did you stay there? If you felt sick after you left the party, why not come back to the IMAX? I could have helped you. You may have dropped me like a bad habit, but I would have taken you back.

This is your fault, Lexi. If you had listened to me, if you had trusted me, this never would have happened. But you had to believe Goldman. You thought I was the liar. Well, now you know. I may have lied, but not like him.

Ginger says I failed you. She doesn't know a goddamned thing.

Come on, Lexi! It's been five minutes. Why aren't you responding to the drugs?

You have to respond to the drugs.

You know what, Lex? If you wake up, I'll let them go. That's the deal. If you get better, they can go free and do whatever they want. Call the senator, jump out a window, it doesn't matter to me. But first, Lexi, you have to wake up.

You should have stuck with me, Lex. Look where I am now, and look where you are. I survived, am surviving.

I know, I know. You never would have gone in for this. You chose Burton's *Batman*—I'm with Nolan: *The Dark Knight*. You would have balked the first time we had to kick some teeth in to get more food. No way you would have eaten a guinea pig. No way you would have done the things I had to do to make sure that we survived.

Come on, Lex. Wake up. Your friend gave me this stuff. She called it a cure. Just open your eyes. Something. Anything. Some small sign of life and I'll let them go.

If you're just going to die, why'd I bother dragging your ass down here to this Caddy? I could have just left you in that stockroom. Maybe your friends would have found you—eventually. Hell, if I'd left you alone entirely, you'd be with your mom, safe in the HomeMart. You would never have come to that party. You would never have gotten sick.

But you wanted to be with me, right? You could have left me alone. I was good at alone.

What did I know about friends? What did I know about anything?

Fine, I admit it. I was a bad friend to you. I asked you to do favors for me, to take chances for me, then lied to your face. I screwed you over, Lexi.

There, I said it. Now wake up. Wake up, and I'll give you one free shot at me. Wake up and you can punch me in the face.

This isn't a cheap offer, Lex, not with how fried my face is. I can't open my mouth or even breathe without pain. It hurts to swallow. And no way this heals normal. Punch or no punch, I'm going to be a freak for the rest of my life.

The thing about you, Lexi? You wouldn't care about that. You *liked* the freak in me. Hell, *you're* a freak. You play Minecraft, for Christ's sake. You know how to hotwire a magnetically sealed door.

The freak in you is what I liked too. God knows what you saw in me. It certainly wasn't what you saw on the outside that kept you coming back. I mean, let's be honest—we can be honest now—I wasn't much to look at, even before I turned into Two-Face. When you kissed me, it was dark. If there had been lights, you probably would have come to your senses before you closed the deal.

Would you have, Lex? Would you still have kissed me?

Wake up, Lexi. Please, wake up.

"Marco?"

It's Rafe. I slip out of the car and close the door, returning Lexi to the dark. "What?"

"There's some kind of fire," he says. "The third floor is filling with smoke. Mike says we have to go down a floor, but we haven't gotten word from Heath that the Green Faces are cleared out."

"They're as good as cleared out," I say, grabbing his arm and heading up the stairs two at a time. "Where's the fire?"

"Mike says Baxter's."

How the hell does Mike know this? And why did he not tell me about the fire before it's choking us out?

"So we have some time," I say. Baxter's is half a mall away from us.

We'll move the weapons first, then we find a new command center. Hopefully before the fire burns all our food to a crisp.

Just when everything's coming together, some snag has to come in and rip my carefully wrought masterpiece to shit.

SHAY

BOWLING ALLEY

M arco just walked out on us. Not a word. Just left.

"There's a back door," I say.

"On it." Ginger crosses the room to the short door marked PINSETTER.

It opens to some sort of catwalk spanning the glittering maze of machinery that covers the floor. And on the catwalk is a guard, whose headlamp whips around and blinds me. "Going somewhere?" she asks.

We close the door. Back in our room, I climb on top of a tool chest tucked between spare parts to check the drop ceiling.

"No go," I say. "The wall extends up into a cloud of smoke."

"Then we go out the front door," Ginger says.

We hear Marco on the other side shouting orders in the hallway.

"He'll come back for us," I say, eyeing the tool chest.

"No doubt," Ginger says.

There's nothing weapon-like in the chest. Marco's gang must have cleaned it out long ago. All we find is a tape measure. Ginger pockets it.

"I need the mask," Ginger says, hand out, and I take it out of my bag.

"You wait by the door," she says, putting the mask on. She then climbs up into the drop ceiling.

As expected, Marco does not leave without saying good-bye.

"Shay," he says as he walks through the door.

Ginger drops down onto him and I shut the door so none of his thug friends can see.

"You're going to walk us out of here," Ginger says, crouched on top of him, the metal strip from the tape measure held taut across his throat.

Marco elbows her in the chest, but Ginger doesn't even flinch. She digs her knee into his spine.

"I was coming to let you out," he says, gasping.

"Right," I say, peeking out the door. Headlamps slice the air like a laser show. The gang is shouting at one another; no one would notice if Marco screamed. There's a door across the hall marked FIRE. "We'll take the stairs," I say to Ginger.

She pulls the nail gun from Marco's homemade holster and slides it across the floor to me. Then she drags him by the throat to his feet.

"Seriously," he says. "You don't have to do this."

"One more word," Ginger says, "and I will choke you."

The headlampers seem more interested in running

down the hall than in watching us, so we cross into the
fire stairwell without incident. Marco doesn't even fight
us as we stumble down through the darkness, pushing
him out front in case the place is booby-trapped.

We reach the first floor.

"Keep going," Marco says. "Go to the parking garage."

"Yeah," Ginger says. "Let's follow the killer's advice."

"Please," Marco says. He sounds so earnest, I almost
want to believe him.

"Did they take your flashlight?" I ask Ginger. The
service hall beyond the door is pitch-black and I'm sick
of being jumped.

"Yeah," Ginger says. "You have a light, tough guy?"
The tape measure clicks tighter.

"I'm clean out," he says. "I will help you, but you have
to go to the parking garage."

Do we want any kind of help Marco could offer?

"I could have gotten away from you at any point," he
says. "But I'm still here."

"What's in the garage?" Ginger asks.

"My gang's last-ditch escape plan."

We go down the last flight of steps with Ginger still
holding Marco by the throat.

"You open it," I say to Marco when we reach the door.

The handle squeals. The parking garage is as dark as
the stairs, the air still and musty as a tomb.

"Walk forward about twenty feet," he says.

We do, pushing him out in front of us, until he
stops.

"Open the rear door."

My fingers feel smooth metal, then glass—a car door? I find and lift the handle, and the car's interior light pierces the dark. There's a body in the backseat.

"Lexi!" Ginger shouts. I hear the metal strip snap back into the tape measure. Marco's free.

Ginger climbs into the car's backseat. Marco stashed a dead body in the car, and Ginger is now hugging it.

"Don't hurt her," Marco says, pulling Ginger off.

"What did you do to her?" Ginger growls.

"I saved her life," he says, and shoves Ginger out of the car. She just stands there, stunned.

Marco lifts the girl—Lexi—in his arms and carries her to one of several motorcycles standing in an odd formation just to the right of the door to the fire stairwell. "You can drive this across the mall to the HomeMart. My only condition is that you take her with you." He slides Lexi's leg over the seat, then sits her gently against the cushioned metal backrest.

"Either of you ever ridden a motorcycle?" he asks. As he speaks, he pulls off the harness he had the nail gun in and slips it over Lexi's head, strapping her to the bike.

"My cousin's moped in India," I say.

"Probably the same kind of thing," Marco says. "One of my guys hotwired all these for us. In terms of riding, from what my boy says, you just squeeze the clutch, which is this metal bar here—"

"I can manage this," I say. It's enough like the moped that I can get us across a parking lot.

He looks up at me. "I still think your plan sucks."

"I don't care what you think."

Ginger slips onto the seat between me and Lexi. "Let's go."

Marco hands me a walkie-talkie. "It's the one we took off the cop, like a hundred years ago when we got our all-access key card," he says. "I saved some battery, for what, I have no idea. Maybe it will help get you inside."

I pass the walkie-talkie to Ginger, then check the bike's in neutral and turn it on. I want to ride away, but that feels wrong. I can't think of anything else to say, so I say, "Thanks."

He winces half a smile, then nods. "Yeah." He takes a step back toward the door, pauses to brush a piece of hair from Lexi's mouth. "I hope you make it."

Hope. For all the asshole posturing, Marco hopes.

"The mall offices," I say. It's a chance, but I decide to take it. "Preeti's in there. She's sick, and there are others. If the fire gets bad, please help move them."

Marco sighs, continues toward the door. "I can't promise anything."

It's done. He'll do whatever he's going to do.

"Hold on," I say to Ginger. I let out the clutch and we roll into the dark.

MARCO

PARKING GARAGE

Shay's motorcycle is a point of light in the black. I did everything I could to save you, Lexi. Not that you'll know about it.

Back to phase two.

It looked like the gang had cleared the weapons room as instructed, so now it's just a matter of wiping out the green-face threat and securing a new command center on the second floor.

No sense walking into battle when you can ride. I grab the nearest bike, start the thing up, then navigate my way to the central pavilion. Mike told me he punched an SUV through the glass, so I easily make it to the steps. Heath gave us a lesson on riding, but this is the first time I'm really doing it. The engine buzzes between my thighs; the wheels scream on the tile. I bounce up onto the first floor.

Funny, this all started with Mike and a bike. Ha! It rhymes.

I am a comet, blasting down the hall, swerving around crap, my headlight carving tunnels of light through the dark to the escalator. The bike flies off the top step onto the second floor.

Down the hall, the food court is on fire. Meaning the second floor might not be the best place for a new command center. Scanning the floor above, I see most of the third floor from the T. J. O'Flannigan's on back is *en fuego*. So we have very little time before we must be cleared out of the bowling alley.

My team is supposed to regroup in the Abercrombie. But as I drive up, the place is a ghost store. I continue down the hall, toward the food court, and discover why.

Anarchy. Mayhem. Garden-variety vandalism. Heath and another guy are torching the horses on the carousel.

"Where the hell is everyone?" I yell, pulling alongside the broken fence that once held a line of squalling kids.

"Here!" Heath yells back, waving his hand, which grips an ax. "At the party at the end of the world!" He returns to chopping the head from one of the ponies.

There's Laila, flinging flaming tennis balls from her slingshot at Donna, one of our own. They're both laughing, even though Donna's hoodie has caught on fire. And there's Jake and Neil dragging some helpless douchebags from a store. Where's the discipline? What about the freaking plan?

And then I see Mike standing over a girl he just felled

with one swipe of a bat. He's laughing, even as I see a guy slam him in the back with a two-by-four.

If they think I'm giving up, giving in to this place, they are insane.

I gun the engine, stall, restart the damn thing, and fly toward the escalator. I jump onto the third floor and ride into my bowling alley, down my hall, to my stockpile of food.

The smoke is so thick, I can barely breathe. I heft the bucket of dried eggs, and get five feet before I'm sucking wind.

How could they give up? After everything we've been through, everything we've done to get here?

I drag that damn bucket to the front of the bowling alley. My lungs burn—screw my lungs, I keep going. Haul the box of chips, the crate of water. Only when I cut my hand open on the edge of a flat and there's no one to catch the pallet before it drops onto my boot do I admit it: I am no longer good at alone.

The entrance to the bowling alley glows orange as I approach out of the dark. Human screams, some from pain, some not, compete with the voiceless roar of the fire. It's close enough for me to feel its heat.

I get on the bike and ride across the hall, down the hallway, and stop in front of the mall offices.

"Ryan?" I yell, punching open the door.

A metal pole whacks me across the chest.

"Get the hell out!" the douche screams.

"Shay told me to come here," I say. "She asked me to—"

The punch glances off my cheekbone, scraping the charred flesh of my skin, and I black out.

Water splashes across my skin and Ryan shakes me back to life. "Can you ride that bike?"

"So much of me wants to kill you right now." I push my body upright. My cheek pulses with pain.

"We have to move these people," he says, shuffling down the hall. "And I don't know how to work a motor-cycle."

A half-dead book light hangs from a ceiling tile and illuminates several prone bodies. Ryan backs out of the dark at the end of the hall, dragging a girl by the ankles. "There are four including her who can't walk down," he says, laying her at my feet. "You take them on the bike. I'll follow with the ones who can move on their own."

It's Shay's sister, Preeti. She's sick, probably not going to make it to the end of the day, and really, are any of us?

"Why are you even bothering?" I say. "If you're not burned in the fire, you'll be choked by the smoke. Even on the lower floors, it's just a matter of hours."

"Tell me now if you've given up," he says. "I'm moving these people with or without you." He shuffles on his makeshift crutch back into the dark.

I hate him more now than ever.

But I still lift the girl in my arms, place her on my bike, then go back to get another.

GINGER

S hay stops the bike when the headlamp finds solid
wall. She twists the handlebars, scanning the
concrete with the beam until she finds a door
marked FIRE.

"The HomeMart should be up those stairs," she says,
and cuts the engine.

We slip off the bike. Shay leaves the headlight on, so
we're not sucked back into the endless black that sur-
rounds us. I drop the nail gun and walkie-talkie by the
wall, then help Shay carry Lexi across the pavement.

"I'll get the door," Shay says.

The last time I saw Lexi, we'd been doing laundry, the
three of us. Maddie and I left to sample clothes from our
secret closet. I'm still wearing the top she told me to try on.

Marco stole our chance. He took the *one* chance Maddie had and hid it from us in the basement. So our plan

didn't fail, it never could have succeeded in the first place. All because of Marco.

Lexi's eyes flutter, then squint at me. "Ginger?" she whispers.

Tears spill down my cheeks. "We're taking you to your mom," I say.

"Help me!" a voice rasps and a man claws his way into the cone of the headlight.

Shay grabs the nail gun.

"This is almost over," she says to him. "We have no food. Just the bike, which you can have. But we need to go up those stairs to the HomeMart."

"Take me with you," the man says. "Don't leave me."

"We won't leave you," Shay says, taking the man's hand.

Is she insane? He's going to kill us.

But he doesn't. The man takes her hand and begins to cry.

Then she turns to me, smiling. It's like she's seen the future, already knows we make it out.

I nod, and pick up the walkie-talkie.

Shay leaves the nail gun by the bike. We each take a side, shoulder to Lexi's shoulder, and slowly, the shadow guy gripping Shay's hand like a lifeline, make our way up the stairs.

The stairwell lets us out in a service hallway. The first door we come to has the word *HomeMart* spray-painted across it.

Shay goes right up to it and knocks.

"I knocked," the man says. "They didn't answer."

"I'm sure a lot of people have knocked on this door,"

I say. Lexi is heavier than I can manage, and we slump down the wall to the floor.

"I'm sure people haven't knocked, then *called*." Shay takes the walkie-talkie from my hand, clicks on the volume, and squeezes the talk button. "Senator Ross, it's Shaila Dixit. I have Lexi. I'm at the service door. Please let us in."

She releases the button.

The senator's probably long gone by now. The government cleared the adults out, I'm sure, left the rest of us—

"Miss Dixit?"

We lock eyes. Holy crap, she's really still here. It hits me that I never thought this would work, that the whole time, even with Maddie, I thought I was merely stalling Death, not betting on survival.

"Yes!" Shay yells, then remembers to hold the talk button. "Yes," she says again, more calmly. "Senator, we need to talk to you—"

"You have Lexi? She's alive?"

"Yes," she says, giving me the thumbs-up. "We're outside a door on the south side of the store. I need to tell you something. I have Dr. Chen's notes."

There's a pause.

"Wait by the door."

I clutch Lexi to me, hug her so hard that even in her near-comatose state she weakly swats at me and whispers, "Too tight."

Something in the door clunks. It opens. The senator stumbles out into the dark. "Shaila?" A lantern flickers to life. The senator's face is haggard. Her hair is a spiky nest. "Miss Dixit?"

Behind her is more darkness. Shouldn't there be light?
People? I think I hear banging.

"Where is everyone?" Shay asks.

"They're trying to escape, have been for hours. At this
point, it's just something to do," she says. Then she turns
to me. "Lexi!" she cries, and falls to her knees.

She throws her arms around her daughter and catches
me in the hug too. My body starts shaking with sobs. I
don't even feel sad, I'm just crying, like my brain still has
to catch up.

"I have Dr. Chen's notes," Shay says, interrupting. "Do
you still have some connection to the government outside?"

The senator releases me, keeps one hand on Lexi like
she could disappear at any moment. "Thank you for bringing her. I didn't think I'd get to say good-bye." She smiles
at Shay like Lexi's already dead. "Here," she says, and
pulls the satellite phone I'd seen her with back in the
normal mall from a pocket. "You can call, but they won't
answer. I've been leaving messages for days. At least you
both can say good-bye to your families."

And I thought I'd been blown away before. My chest
sucks inward, but it's not breath, it's just that I'm completely shattered.

Shay takes the phone. "They'll answer my call," she
says, and hits the call button.

She waits, and I hear the recording. Shay gazes into the
lantern light, then speaks. "My name is Shaila Dixit. I have
the notes of Dr. Chen from the CDC." She explains about the
mutation. That we're not a threat anymore. Then hangs up.

"Do you know what happened to Dr. Chen?" the senator asks.

"Someone shot him," Shay says.

The senator nods like she expected it.

Shay calls again. She tells about how Dr. Chen must have figured all this stuff about the mutation out right before he died, that he must have tested his idea on her because she was coughing blood, hours from death herself, when she got to the med center, but she lived. She's the proof he was right. She hangs up.

"I'm so sorry," the senator says. She holds Lexi, and it's not clear which of us she's speaking to.

Shay calls again. She tells them she started a fire in the bookstore and that it's spread. That the whole mall will burn to the ground with everyone inside it, and that it doesn't have to be that way. That they could save us. That all they have to do is pick up the phone.

She started the fire? And Marco stole Lexi out from under us. The senator locked us out in the mall, the government locked us in here. They all screwed us, Maddie. Everyone let us down.

"My next call is to 911," Shay says, leaving yet another message. "I will tell them everything I told you, and ask that they share it with whatever news agency will listen. I am not letting this place go down without a fight."

The man from the basement crawls into the circle of light.

"John?" the senator says. "Goldman said you got separated. I had hoped you survived."

He gives her a pinched smile.

And then the phone rings.

All four of us jump.

"Hello?" Shay says.

We all lean in for the answer.

M A R C O

MALL OFFICES AND PET STORE

carry Preeti and another kid down to the first floor on my bike. The pet store is near the escalator and looks empty, so I stash them in there in a dog bed. As I ride back up to get the next invalid, I pass Ryan and the gimps fumbling down the steps through the smoke.

"I put the kids in the pet store," I say, pausing at the top of the stairs.

"There're more in the back room on the right."

The book light in the hall looks like a lighthouse locked in fog, the smoke's so thick. I haul the girl closest to the door out into the hall. The air is sticking in my throat. Thank you, Senator, for keeping a supply of face masks handy. I sling on two, but still can barely breathe.

I heft the girl's body onto the bike. One arm on the handlebars, one arm around the girl, we bump and ride down to the first floor.

Ryan's made it down with the crew of the damned. He's setting them up near the cloudy remains of the fish tanks.

"Here's another." I let the kid slide off the bike onto a stack of cat litter bags. She starts to roll off. I stick a leg out and catch her before she hits the tile.

"This is better, right?" Ryan asks as he eases the sick girl off my foot and onto the ground.

"Better than running a crew? Better than kicking everyone's ass? No. This is not better than that."

He shakes his head like I'm such a moron.

"You self-righteous prick," I say. "Like you're not getting off on your moral superiority. Like your bagging Shay doesn't make you feel like the biggest dick in the room. In the immortal words of Mel Brooks, *It's good to be the king,* and you know it."

"It feels good to help people, yeah," he says, dragging the girl to a pile of dog jackets near the wall. "But I didn't bag Shay. She's not baggable. Your problem?" He's back in my face. "You're pissed because she chose me over you. You just wanted someone to like you. But who the hell really likes a bully?"

"Screw you." I start the damn bike and roar out of there like a goddamned hurricane.

Screw all of these people. Screw the whole goddamned mall. Screw this fire. Screw the smoke. I rev the bike and just ride and ride. As a wall looms, I turn up the stairs and fly the other way.

Holy crap. The whole second floor is just people running, screaming. Some are trying to get down out of the smoke, but most have joined in the bedlam my old crew ignited in the food court. That place is like a mosh pit.

Bodies slam into one another. Punches fly. Hair is pulled. They don't even seem to notice the fire.

I keep riding. I bump up the stairs and park outside the mall offices and slink inside like the asshole I am and grab the next sick douche in the lineup.

As I drag his limp body down the hall, the front door handle rattles.

No one I want to run into would be coming in here. I drop the guy's arms. What the hell is weaponizable in this place?

"I saw you come in here, Headlamp."

Holy shit, it's Knife-fist. This guy won't die!

The nearest door opens into an office crammed with useless computers. I duck in, grab a flat screen, and wait. He steps into the doorway.

I smash him in the face with the screen and drive him back down the hall.

He swipes at me with his armored knuckles, catches the good side of my face. I duck, and the blades scrape up my cheek. He knees me in the gut, kicks my calf.

"Told you I would kill you," he says.

I catch him in a headlock. "You'll have to try harder than that."

He pulls me onto his back and drags me into the reception room, then spins and slams my spine against the wall, squeezing the air from my lungs. I lose my grip on him. Knife-fist thrusts away from my body, turns, pulls back his arm to nail me with his claws.

I tackle him. He falls onto the reception desk. I pin his arms with my knees. His head hits the window frame Heath broke forever ago. I crawl on top of him. This all started because of him. My hands wrap around his neck. Everything was fine before his people started the stupid war. I have him over the edge of the window frame. I had a gang before he broke them apart. Shards of broken glass cut his skin, and his blood runs over my fingers.

He's glaring up at me.

Then his face changes.

His eyes widen. Mouth falls open.

He's afraid.

Knife-fist, afraid?

Of what?

Of *me.*

I start to sweat. He's not moving. His head lolls over the edge of the window frame. I'm sweating so much, it's running off my scalp, down my forehead, across my nose. Drops fall onto Knife-fist's dead face. I hate this guy. He tried to kill me. And yet I pull away so I don't drip on him. The sweat hits my burned cheek and the skin flares anew. Snot runs out of my nose.

I crawl off Knife-fist and stumble back into the mall.

Then somewhere outside, thunder booms.

An explosion?

Does it matter?

Glass shatters. Light, brighter than a thousand head-lamps, shines down from above.

The central skylight has dropped inward. Black smoke belches out into clear blue.

It's sunlight. It's blinding.

The sick guy I dragged from the back has risen from the dead and finds me.

"Is it—?" he asks, arm shielding his eyes from the strip of sunlight. I guess he's too afraid to say *over*.

It doesn't feel over.

"Attention, shoppers." The voice is alien, shouting down at us like a god.

Can they seriously be calling us shoppers?

The sky is so blue, it seems fake. Using my hand as a visor, I scan the rim of black ceiling and find a person clad in a blue hazmat suit holding a megaphone perched on the edge of the roof.

"May I have your attention."

Like we're paying attention to anything else.

"The quarantine has been suspended. Emergency fire and rescue personnel have been brought in to control the blaze. Please make your way to the central courtyard. We are working on an exit strategy."

Mike.

I need Mike.

I stumble forward, out of the mall offices, down the escalator, and run for the food court. I step over a girl whose leg is bent the wrong way. Two kids stand frozen mid-fight, fists gripping each other's clothing, and stare up at the tear in our universe.

"Smell the air?" one says.

"It's cold," replies the other.

"Mike!" I yell.

Some people are crying. Some are running toward the escalators, racing to the central courtyard, desperate to be processed. Some reach a hand out to help those who can't run on their own.

"Mike!" I scream.

He's not near the carousel or the twisted remains of the Ferris wheel. I look across the food court, past the stream of people. A shadow moves in the billowing smoke on the other side.

"Mike!"

The smoke and flames blow sideways, first one way, then the other, as the clean air flows down and the hot, dead air of the mall rushes out. A cloud separates and I catch Mike's legs, then his body, then his elbow, bent.

Glock barrel against his head.

"Don't you dare!" My words catch. Tears shred my face.

He stumbles deeper into the smoke.

I chase him into the atrium.

"Get away from me," he says, still holding the gun to his head.

"We walk out of here together."

He pushes me away. "Tell them I had the flu."

I punch him in the gut, and make a grab for the gun.

The gunshot is deafening. My hand feels like it's been ripped in two.

"What the hell?" Mike rasps.

I fall to my knees, tuck my hand into my belly. So much pain. But also no pain, just a fizz, my whole body dissolving.

Mike grabs my shoulder, shakes me hard. "I only had the one bullet," he yells. "I was saving it!"

"You shot me," I say.

"I was fucking saving it!"

The smoke is thick, and I can't see his face.

"I can't walk out of here without you," I say.

Mike lets go of my shoulder. I hear footsteps. He's leaving me.

Then the smoke shifts. And Mike is wrapping my hand in something. He didn't leave. I drop my head against his chest.

When I come to, he is dragging me, my arm slung across his shoulders, out into the light.

THREE
WEEKS
LATER

WSCL Channel 9 News
November 22, 20_ 09:30 A.M. EST

KYRA HUNTLEY, WSCL REPORTER: Good morning, I'm here at the Shops at Stonecliff to witness the demolition of what was once the twenty-fifth-largest mall in the country. With me are hundreds of observers, including some of the people who only three weeks ago were trapped inside this gigantic structure.

(BEGIN VIDEO CLIP: Exterior Perimeter, Shops at Stonecliff 11/22/-- 08:34 A.M. EST)

UNIDENTIFIED WOMAN: I had to come back. I had to see the end of this.

HUNTLEY: Did you lose someone inside?

UNIDENTIFIED WOMAN: Didn't we all?

(END CLIP)

The quarantine inside the mall officially ended on Tuesday, November first, after nearly three weeks of continuous confinement for the thousands of innocent workers and shoppers who were inside when a bomb went off, releasing a deadly virus. Government officials terminated the quarantine after being

notified that a fire was burning out of
control in the top floor of the complex.
Families camped outside the perimeter fence,
this twenty-foot tall, electrified and razor-
wire topped wall behind me, were uprooted
to allow entry to scores of fire trucks and
emergency vehicles. Helicopters dumped
water on the roof above Baxter's Books,
where authorities indicated the fire started.
The government maintains its denial that this
fire was part of a plan to exterminate the
quarantined people, thereby eliminating
the deadly flu.

Even as fire and rescue teams attempted to
control the blaze, teams from the Centers
for Disease Control worked to save the people
trapped inside.

(BEGIN VIDEO CLIP: Helicopter footage,
Exterior Shops at Stonecliff 11/1/-- 2:00
P.M. EST)

The mall's original entrances were sealed
at the start of the quarantine, and so narrow
openings had to be punched into the concrete
bunkers. Representatives from the CDC donned
hazmat suits to receive each person as they
were evacuated. Individuals were stripped
of their ragged clothing, then escorted
into showers where they were sprayed with

disinfectant. After leaving the showers, survivors were conducted under a large pavilion of tents set up on the parking lot grounds.

Onlookers were astonished to see the haggard shoppers stagger out into the afternoon sun. Many of those released held hands up to their eyes, as if they'd been in darkness for an extended period of time. The survivors' skin also looked dirty, like they were covered in soot, and their clothes were black and torn.

(END CLIP)

HUNTLEY: I have here with me Jillian Foster, who survived the mall and came back to witness its demolition. Good morning, Ms. Foster.

JILLIAN FOSTER: Good morning.

HUNTLEY: What brought you back here today?

FOSTER: I needed to see it destroyed. I needed to be here, to witness it for myself. I think it will help me feel like I'm really out of there.

HUNTLEY: Are you saying you still feel like you're inside the mall?

FOSTER: Some part of me will always be inside that mall.

HUNTLEY: Thank you. Here is another man who has come to witness the demolition. Sir, were you confined in the mall?

KEITH ROSENMAN: (*Unintelligible, staring off-camera.*)

HUNTLEY: I'm sorry, could you repeat that?

KEITH ROSENMAN: It's such a big place. They say they searched everywhere, but it's so big.

HUNTLEY: Yes . . . sir . . . Thank you.
(*Walks away.*)
    For an additional two weeks, the survivors were held for treatment and processing on site in the parking lot surrounding the mall. CDC officials, including Director Lillian Knight, claimed that they were being monitored for any signs of infection. She had this to say at the time:

(BEGIN VIDEO CLIP: Press Tent, Perimeter — Shops at Stonecliff 11/1/-- 1:55 P.M. EST)

LILLIAN KNIGHT, DIRECTOR, CENTERS FOR DISEASE CONTROL AND PREVENTION: Although we

have deemed it safe to allow the quarantined
individuals to leave the confines of the mall
itself, we are not yet ready to allow them to
have contact with the outside world. Doctors
on the premises will monitor all the
survivors for signs of infection over
the next fourteen days, which is the maximum
incubation period observed for this virus.
In addition, any individuals exhibiting signs
of illness or injury will be held indefinitely
until our doctors clear them for reentry into
the general population.

(END CLIP)

HUNTLEY: During this time, visitors were
denied contact with the survivors, which
led to several altercations with the National
Guard who maintained the perimeter around the
mall. Many families were angry that the government failed to release the names of the
dead as soon as they were identified. Others
complained that anyone who had been injured
during the course of the quarantine should
be visited by legal counsel before treatment
so that the extent of their injury could be
documented for future lawsuits.

This complaint was addressed by John
Fletcher, Deputy Director of the Department
of Homeland Security and point person for the
quarantine management team.

(BEGIN VIDEO CLIP: Press Tent, Perimeter —
Shops at Stonecliff 11/5/-- 2:30 P.M. EST)

DEPUTY FLETCHER: All of those recorded as
having been a part of this quarantine, whether
detained in the primary quarantine site, or
held under house arrest, have been offered a
settlement with respect to any and all legal
claims associated with their internment. These
reparations are being given on the condition
that the individual or their estate waive any
and all claims against the government and its
agents, and the mall and individual stores,
regarding the quarantine, and that the survivors
sign a non-disclosure agreement.

In offering these reparations, we hope to
compensate these innocent victims of terrorism
for any lost wages or other costs incurred as
a result of the quarantine, bringing a swift
resolution to a trying time in the nation's
history.

In addition, the events of the actual
quarantine have been classified as a matter
of national security. Participants in the
quarantine have been apprised of the sensitive
nature of the procedures employed during the
quarantine. These procedures will be reviewed
to prepare us in the event of another attack
of this nature. Maintaining a level of security around this information may help us in
that unfortunate event.

(END CLIP)

HUNTLEY: When those quarantined were finally let out of the perimeter, one week ago, it was a scene of overwhelming joy for those families reunited with their loved ones. For the survivors, it was a long-overdue trip home, though some individuals who required continued care were instead transferred to permanent medical facilities for the duration of their recovery. For many, however, the day brought nothing but grief.

Before the detainees were released, families of those who did not survive were contacted privately. A complete list of casualties was later distributed to the public. We will be running the list of those dead at the end of this broadcast.

The list provoked confusion and outright denial, much of this fueled by the CDC's decision not to release the remains of the victims. Lillian Knight again:

(BEGIN VIDEO CLIP: Press Tent, Perimeter — Shops at Stonecliff 11/15/-- 12:35 P.M. EST)

DIRECTOR KNIGHT: Unfortunately, to ensure that the original Stonecliff Flu virus remains contained, we have determined that none of the bodies can be removed from the premises. Any individuals who passed away either during the quarantine or post-quarantine detainment

period will be cremated on site. The quarantine
facility, formerly the Shops at Stonecliff,
will be destroyed in its entirety. Given the
public health risk, it will not be possible
to individually confirm the identities of the
dead.

I understand that this will be difficult for
many of you. This was a difficult choice for
us to make. But the safety of the population
at large is of paramount importance. I extend
my condolences to all the families receiving
bad tidings today.

(END CLIP)

HUNTLEY: I have with me Keith and Debbie
Rosenman. They lost their daughter, Diane,
during the quarantine. In lieu of a funeral,
the Rosenmans invited family and friends to
witness the demolition.

(*Turns to Rosenmans*) I'm so sorry for your
loss. I understand your daughter was a college
student at a nearby university?

DEBORAH ROSENMAN: Yes, she was studying fashion
design. She came to the mall every weekend.
She called it studying, and even if it wasn't
the cheapest course of study for us, it allowed
her to express her passions. She had her own
style, and she was never afraid to show it.
(*Shows framed portrait.*)

My husband and I decided to hold the funeral
today, here, seeing as this will be her last
resting place. But it was also a special place
to her. We wanted to be here for her, to say
good-bye.

HUNTLEY: The Rosenmans are not alone in
this sentiment. We have confirmed that
at least seventy-five different funeral
services have been conducted this morning
on the grounds.

KEITH ROSENMAN: (*Interrupting*) Diane played
hockey. She was a tough girl—gentle, still
Daddy's girl, but tough. And she never got
sick. Diane was a survivor. I can't believe
she wouldn't have survived.

HUNTLEY: I'm so sorry, Mr. Rosenman. Thank
you for your time.
    John Fletcher, Deputy Director of the Depart-
ment of Homeland Security, has stepped up to
the press podium.

DEPUTY FLETCHER: Good morning. Since the
beginning of the quarantine, the FBI has
been coordinating with local and state
law enforcement in the investigation
of the attack on the mall. Early on, all
relevant evidence was recovered from the
scene, including the bomb used in the attack

and samples of the virus taken from inside
the mall's ventilation ducts, as well as
surveillance tapes from both the mall and
surrounding buildings. This evidence has been
under evaluation by top investigative teams.
Preliminary findings have resulted in promising
leads that are being pursued by teams in the
field.

After the end of the quarantine and the
mall's evacuation, teams in protective suits
initiated a room-by-room search of the entire
facility with assistance from rescue dogs
and thermal-imaging technology. Any survivors
were identified and removed from the building.
We have confirmed that any and all living
people have been evacuated from the
structure.

UNIDENTIFIED MALE: You can't be sure!

HUNTLEY: I believe that was Keith Rosenman?

DEPUTY FLETCHER: Sir, please do not interrupt.
Yes, we are sure. We have taken every measure
to ensure that every living being has been
removed from the building.

With respect to the demolition of the
structure itself, the process is two-fold. To
ensure that all biological remains within the

mall are incinerated, a powerful incendiary
device will be set off inside the mall. To
demolish the building itself, a second series
of explosives will be detonated. These explosives
are the more common ones used in the demolition
of structures.

To honor those who lost their lives during
the quarantine, we invite New York State
Senator Dorothy Ross to initiate the detona-
tion. Senator Ross was instrumental in both
containing the initial threat posed by the
bomb, and in maintaining order during the
course of the quarantine. We thank you for
your service. The demolition will now
commence.

HUNTLEY: The clock behind Deputy Fletcher has
lit up with a countdown. Ten seconds, nine.
Wait, Charlie, change the shot, over there!
A car has just crashed through the fence near
the gate!

MECHANICAL ANNOUNCEMENT: *FIVE, FOUR*

HUNTLEY: Someone, stop the countdown!

THREE

There's a man in the

TWO

perimeter!

ONE

(END CLIP)

LEXI

CHAT WITH D-MASTER

> **Guess who?**

> If it isn't Lexi Ross.
> You were released how long ago
> and you're only texting me now?

> **I was busy recovering from almost dying.**
> **Then my mom had to get me a new phone,**
> **and I had to convince the ICU people to let me**
> **use it. The Senator had to pull rank, I think.**
> **It's been a whole thing.**

> I'll think about forgiving you.

> **How long is that going to take?**

Let's see. Five, four, three, two—
Forgiven.
When are you coming home?

Not sure. ICU people are all nervous.
They keep checking my machines,
taking notes, frowning.

Not cool. Want me to rescue you?

Not sure rescuing is the best idea.
Might actually still be in need of
medical attention.

Want a visitor?

A visitor would be nice ☺

R Y A N

Bleacher seats suck. Sitting on the hard, cold metal in the November breeze feels like being on a shelf in a meat locker. I haven't watched a football game from the bleachers in years, and never a Turkey Bowl game.

I quit the team. I've told everyone who asks, I *quit*. I wasn't kicked off. It wasn't because of my ankle.

Newspapers, real newspapers from New York City, have interviewed me about all sorts of crap—my prospects as a high school player, how I was set to get a Big Ten scholarship offer (news to me), why I refused to do a Sportade endorsement deal, how my exercise regimen before the attack made me more likely to survive, details about my football career as a nobody wide receiver in a crap league in upstate New York.

The announcer calls that West Nyack won the toss and has elected to receive the kickoff. I watch as Thad gets his guys into formation. They replaced me with Tim Yancy. Tim Yancy can't run for shit.

Obviously, I still care about the team. My brother's the quarterback. I know all these guys. So, yeah, it bugs me that the coach picked Yancy. Yancy sucks.

My ankle still looks like crap. They had to graft on some skin and the whole thing looks like a bad makeup job in a horror movie. Some of the muscle was affected, gangrene or something. I can walk, though I feel the weakness if I try to run on it. Still, Monday I go back to school.

John Reisman catches the kick and is downed at the West Nyack forty-five. Not a bad place. Thad will try to toss a dart to Yancy. There's the snap—too long in the hand, bro. And Yancy's too slow getting out, he can't get his head around to see the pass. The ball slides right through his fingers.

My father is on his feet screaming that the ref screwed up. But it's clear this is on Yancy. Thad and I drilled that pattern all season. I would have made that catch.

But Dad's yelling that a defender was offside, like Yancy didn't clearly botch the play. That's Dad. Completely wrong, and still shouting. He and Mom are down at the bottom of the bleachers, near the field. They're always there, every game. Mom told me I could sit with them. I didn't want to be so obvious.

Turns out, Mom spent the whole time I was in the mall praying. She moved into her church. Dad got so sick of waiting for dinner he started eating out every night at the local bar. Thad stayed out with guys from the team, would eat at their houses.

Everything's changed now that I'm back. Even though Thad's busy with college applications and interviews and tryouts, he sits with me to watch TV for a few hours every day. Dad still hits the bar during the day—with the settlement the government's paying out to all the survivors, he has decided to take a "vacation." I heard my parents fighting that first night. Mom tried to tell Dad that it was my money, that it was for college, but he argued that he'd been paying for me for fifteen years, and I owed him—but he's home every night at five thirty. He's stinking drunk, but he's there. Every evening, Dad stumbles in, drops his butt into the seat at the head of the table, turns his bloodshot eyes to me, and asks how my day was.

Mom's doting on me twenty-four/seven like some invalid. She makes me lunch and brings it to me on a tray with a folded napkin. She comes into my room in the morning, opens the curtains, and says things like, "We should let some sunshine in. You miss sunshine, don't you?"

I've been taking walks to avoid being smothered. Mom doesn't question it because the doctors told me I have to work my new skin to keep it flexible. I tried hanging out in a nearby park and just sitting on the swings in the cold, but I don't like being exposed like that, so I've been hiding in the town library. The place is pretty shabby. I wanted to read some of those poems from Shay's book, so I searched the shelves for Tagore, but the librarian said they don't have any.

Last night, my mother surprised me with a visit from her priest. Dad turned off the TV, and all four of us sat in front of the guy and chatted nicely while Mom spooned out wet slabs of lasagna. He was nice enough, said a short grace and thanked us for opening our home to him. After dinner, over pie, he said he just wanted to check in with me. I told him I was fine, that everything was fine. When he left, I went into my room and closed the door and just stared at the wall.

Next play, Thad tries to run it himself, which is dumb because he's seen that Ossining's defensive line is like the Great Wall of China. He's just showing off for the recruiters, hoping they'll see he has guts. I think they'll see he's trying to show off.

When I got out, Thad was weird. He'd heard that Drew was dead. Mike must have told him. Mike got out with the main group from the parking lot. I was transferred to a hospital for a few extra days because I tested positive for a blood infection. No one with any signs of infection was allowed back into the world until they were cleared by CDC staff.

I'm guessing Thad is pissed because of what I said when he and my parents picked me up from the hospital—first words out of my mouth: that I was no longer playing ball. Football is all we've ever done together. There's the stuff with Dad, but it's not something we talk about.

Third down and Coach tries to stretch the field by having Yancy run a fly route, but the defense goes for Thad. He doesn't even try to throw the ball away and gets sacked. Not good to have this many screw-ups in your first possession.

Kicker shanks the punt, and our offensive side leaves the field, heads hung low. Thad snaps the chin strap on his helmet, slams the thing onto the bench. West Nyack defense heads onto the field. Before Thad sits, he glances up. Mom waves and he nods back. He looks around a little more—he's looking for me, I bet—but then he catches Jocelyn Blake's eye and it's clear he's just setting things up for later tonight.

The first night I was home, Thad came into my room late. I was still up. I'm having trouble sleeping.

"What was it like?" he asked. He knew from the news that we had spent our last days in darkness—the government couldn't keep the media from learning that. Little else has gotten out about our time under quarantine. We all had to sign non-disclosure agreements to get the money offered as a settlement. I only know of one person who didn't accept the settlement—this girl Ginger who helped Shay get us all out.

I could have told Thad everything. Maybe Mike already had, maybe this was just a courtesy call. I shrugged. "It sucked," was all I could muster.

Our defensive line is suffering. Ossining's deep in our territory. They fake a pass down the right side of the field, hand off to the running back—who's completely open, not a West Nyack player in sight—and he takes it in for a touchdown. The whole team seems screwed up without Mike and Drew to kick people into line. Mike's taken a leave of absence from school, and his old life, it seems. I haven't seen him since the mall.

It's weird how the mall seems like real life and this life, actual reality, feels fake.

When they ended the quarantine, the blood infection had started to take me down. A guy in a hazmat suit pulled me out of the pet store along with the others Kris and I saved. I came to on a gurney under a tent with a woman in a hazmat suit dabbing my ankle with some gauze. I asked her what happened, and she said, "You made it, kid."

My ankle needed to heal, and I needed to rest, so they gave me pain killers and a sedative and antidepressants and whatever else they thought would keep me on that gurney. Those of us marked as potentially infectious were segregated in sealed tents—Kris was one tent over—but Shay, Claire, Joe, and even Ruthie—she made it, another person I saved—all stood outside my tent and waved to me through the see-through window in the wall in front of my bed.

Ossining kicks it through the goal posts for the extra point and it's our turn with the ball. Thad is overeager and blows an easy short pass. His focus is shot.

After two weeks in the isolation tent, they transferred me by ambulance to the hospital. As it drove, I lay there next to some other transfer, watching houses flash past the window, and felt crushed. All this normal stuff—cars, a pizza place, billboards—how could I go back to this?

I realized I couldn't. There was no going back. Surviving meant I had to stop faking. Had to stop trying to be Thad or whoever else I'd been pretending to be. I want to be real, I want to feel alive. I know it sounds crazy, but the thing I remember feeling most in the mall is that: alive.

I felt like a freaking god walking out of the hospital. I knew who I was. I loved rock climbing. I loved a girl named Shaila Dixit. I had this crumpled note from Ruthie—a drawing of us in her car, her brother too, with *Thank you* scrawled across the bottom—and was wearing the T-shirt Kris had made for us: "No Dying" in red across my chest. Which is why the first thing out of my mouth was, I'm quitting the team.

What's got me confused is that every morning I wake up feeling more and more lost.

The first quarter ends and we're seven points down. I'm sure Coach is giving it to Thad over his crap passing game. A part of me wants to go down there and tell him to just chill, get his head back in the game. That it doesn't matter who's in the bleachers. If he just plays the way he's always played, a scholarship is in the bag. But I'm sure he doesn't want to hear crap like that from me.

Who Thad needs to hear it from are his two best friends. But they're gone. Drew forever and Mike, well, he's just gone.

It's cloudy and the wind is the kind that sneaks around your jacket. I'm not used to being cold. The mall was always the perfect temperature, until the blackout when it was hot and then hotter.

Evangeline Sawyer climbs the steps of the bleachers. "Weird to see you up here," she says.

"Best view is from the top row." I try to keep my teeth from chattering.

She looks around. "You going to Wes's party later?"

"Maybe I'll stop by." No way I'm going to that party.

She smiles like she knows I'm not going. "Great."

She shuffles down the row on the opposite side of the

stairs and meets up with her friends. I see them lean out to eyeball me. One of them is my ex-girlfriend Emma. I found out from Instagram that she's dating Nate Taylor. We never officially broke up, but from the pictures, she started dating him right after I was locked down. I don't care about that—I left her for Shay. It's that she keeps texting me how sorry she is, and am I okay, and won't it be great to hang out again during free period. I plan on spending all free periods in the crap library.

My phone vibrates and I nearly drop it—I'm still getting used to having a phone again. It's a text from Shay. Her family went on lockdown after she got out—she emailed me, but that was it. Her parents were smothering her in a good way. They all flew back to India for a week for her grandmother's funeral. I have no idea what they burned—nothing got out of the mall that wasn't alive. She was supposed to get back yesterday. This is the first I've heard from her.

I hit the home button and see: *Look down.*

There's nothing under the bleachers.

The phone buzzes in my hand. Shay again: *Not under you. Down.*

I scan the bottom of the bleachers and see her leaning against the railing. She's wearing some big, colorful scarf that whips around like a flag. Her hair swirls in front of her face, which has one of those henna tattoos on it again. I am up and running in a heartbeat.

I nearly collapse into her. "Hi," I say, out of breath.

We lock eyes, lock hands, and it's like the sun has come out.

"Miss me?" she asks.

"Like crazy."

I pull her to me, afraid that if I don't kiss her she'll disappear, and then our lips touch, and I know she's real and I'm real, that this whole thing really happened, and that we're alive and together and it's not until she pulls back and says "You're crying" that I realize I am.

I run a hand across my face, but I don't actually care. "You want to get out of here?" I ask.

"I thought this was a huge game for Thad," she says. "He'd kill you if you left. Plus, I've never seen a football game before."

So we stay. I explain to her everything that's going on and she acts like she's interested. And then it occurs to me that she might really be.

"This isn't boring for you?" I ask.

She looks confused. "I asked you to explain it to me." She nudges me in the shoulder.

"I just figured this would be, like, way below you."

Winding her arm into mine, she says, "This is a part of you, and you are right here next to me."

The second quarter is more of the same from Thad. It's like he's screwing up on purpose. Next play, he calls an audible, fakes a pass, and tries to run it himself. The defense is right there and Thad slides head-first into the tackle—is he trying to get himself killed? I punch my hands deeper into my pockets.

"Something wrong?" Shay asks.

"Thad's having the worst game of his career," I say, kicking the pole of the bench in front of me. "There are scouts here from colleges and he's blowing it."

"You haven't talked to him yet, have you?"

We've been emailing while she's been away. It's been really cool to just send everything in my head to her. She writes back these amazing stories making even breakfast sound like an adventure, and I'm just rambling like an idiot, but she never tells me to shut it. Anyway, this is how she knows I'm still not talking to Thad.

"It's hard," I say.

"No," she says, "it really isn't. You just go down there and open your mouth."

I gaze down the bleachers to where Thad has slumped onto the bench.

"Okay."

It takes me a while to get to the bottom of the bleachers, and then I have to hop the fence to get onto the field and around to where the team is sitting. Some of the guys break into smiles and pat me on the shoulder. I say hi, bump fists and slap backs. It's actually no big deal being down here.

Thad is alone on a bench near the watercooler. I drop next to him.

"You're really sucking," I say.

He looks at me like I just fell from the sky, then goes back to staring at his hands. "Thanks."

"That first day in the mall, before we knew anything, Mike and Drew and me, we got this pick-up game of touch going with some guys from Tarrytown."

"That was right after the game," he says.

"Yeah," I say. "You can imagine how Mike and Drew were looking for payback."

Thad smirks. "Drew knocked out some guy's teeth in that game. Got a flag on the play for unnecessary roughness."

"The Tarrytown guys were all scared shitless of you. Wanted to beat the crap out of me for being a blood relation."

"So did they?"

"They tried." My jaw still hurts and I have a bruised rib from the episode. "Mike and Drew, though; they looked out for me."

Thad slaps his gloves against his palm. "I asked them to," he says. "Before the cell phones were blocked, I texted Mike to cover your ass."

"I know," I say. "Mike made it clear that I was not to leave his sight."

Thad stares out across the field, watching the defensive line continue to screw up. "He didn't say a word to me when he came out," he says. "I learned Drew died from the news."

Now I feel like an ass. "We were there with him, Mike and me," I say. "Drew didn't die alone." I leave out the details. No one needs to know the details.

Thad slaps his gloves again. Somehow the defensive line managed to hold Ossining off to a fourth down. Coach waves for Thad to get the offensive line together.

"You going to Wes's party?" he says, standing.

"Nah," I say.

"You should go," he says, grabbing my shoulder. "Bring that girl you're sitting with. The guys are always asking me about you and I'm sick of making shit up."

"Maybe we'll stop by."

He hefts his helmet and smiles. "Stop by or I tell Mom you coughed."

"Okay, jeez," I say. "We'll stop by."

I turn and feel the smile on my face. Glancing up, I catch Shay staring at me. Her face is a question and she holds a thumb up. I nod, and she flashes this *I-told-you-so* look.

On my way back up to her, I stop in front of my parents. My dad looks away from the players gathering at the West Nyack thirty yard line.

"You all right?" he asks.

"Yeah," I say. "Is it okay if I stop by this party after dinner?" We're doing Thanksgiving at the church.

My mom smiles like I've answered a prayer.

"You need a ride?" my dad asks.

"Thad's got me covered." No way I ride with him.

"She looks nice," my mother says. "Your girlfriend. From the mall, right?"

I catch Shay's face in the crowd. She's watching the game. "She is nice," I say.

"Have fun," my dad adds.

I think he's sober, or at least not drunk. It's the nicest interchange we've had in a long time.

I crawl back up the bleachers, really beginning to feel it in my bum ankle.

"The talk was good?" Shay asks as I settle in beside her.

"All good," I say. "You mind stopping by a party later?"

"Why, Ryan, dear, I thought you'd never ask."

L
E
X
I

CHAT WITH D-MASTER

You free?

Ugh. Mom attack. Gimme sec.

Remind her how important connection with friends is for patients in recovery.

She's become very clingy.

Give the woman a break.

I know, I know. Sheesh, when did you become such a know-it-all? It's just weird, you know? But good weird.

I'll see you at regular visiting hours?

You bringing the Xbox?

Wouldn't dare show up without it.

SHAY

For the thousandth time, Ryan says, "This is my girlfriend, Shay." At first, the words excited me. I've
never been anyone's girlfriend, let alone been introduced that way to popular—and obviously very jealous—
girls. But the excitement wore off fast, and now I feel like
a trophy in Ryan's story—the Triumphant Return of the
Hometown Hero.

I hate myself for begrudging him this party. I want him
to get his life back. He sent me these emails while I was
away detailing his days sitting alone on swings in abandoned playgrounds, roaming the stacks in a dingy library
branch. That's not Ryan.

"Oh. My. God. Shut up, people!" a girl shouts. She's in
front of the TV. Whatever game was playing has been interrupted for this breaking news: They have arrested three
men in connection with the terrorist attack on the Shops

at Stonecliff. The screen shows a dilapidated farmhouse in some desolate patch of grass upstate.

The entire party stops to stare at Ryan and me.

Ryan claps his hands, raises his arms like his team's run one in. "Yes!"

Chatter erupts, a pitter-patter of words in my ears, and Ryan ushers me out of the room, out of the house. We sit on a low rock wall lining a flagstone patio. There is nothing but the wind rattling the branches.

"Why don't I feel anything?" he asks.

And I realize, we've both been faking.

We interrupt this program for breaking news.

"So they caught the people," I say. "It doesn't change what happened."

"But shouldn't this feel good?"

"I'm not sure this news is for us." I gesture toward the window, where inside, someone chants *U—S—A—*, and fists pump the air.

Ryan takes my hand. "It's still good news. It means it's really over."

"It doesn't feel really over."

We sit there, hand in hand, and watch the party until we get too cold and have to go back inside.

Ryan slips into things like he's donning a second skin, smiling and slapping palms. I put on a good face, make nice for the nice people. Around ten o'clock, I get a text from my mother: *I'm outside.* She agreed to let me out of the house on the condition that I agreed to a strict curfew.

"I have to go," I say, tugging on Ryan's hand.

He's all mine again. "Do you need a ride? I can get Thad—"

"My mom's outside," I say.

He pulls me to him. "I don't want to let you go."

I wrap my arms around him, lay my head against his chest, and listen to his lungs, his heart.

He walks me to the door, steps out with me into the night. "Text me later?" he asks.

"I might even call you."

He lowers his lips to mine, and before I can worry too much about my mother's van at the curb, he's kissing me, gently, oh so gently, a wisp of a breath passing between us.

His eyes are full of mischief. "Later, then."

"Yes."

My mother is waiting with the engine running, knuckles white on the steering wheel. Her hands are bonier than before. Bapuji said that she was not able to eat while we were away.

"I'm guessing that is the boy?" she says.

"Ryan."

"He's handsome."

"He is."

She's listening to NPR. *FBI agents used shipping information obtained from a medical supply company to locate the self-proclaimed "Purifiers," who set the bomb in the mall. The company sent a device used for aerosolizing liquids to the address. An FBI spokesperson said earlier that minute fragments of the device were discovered within the original bomb casing. By altering the device to create an ultrafine mist, the terrorists were able to spread the flu virus throughout the mall, infecting the entire population.*

"Can we listen to something else?" I ask.

My mother nods, and I turn the radio off.

We drive in silence, out of West Nyack and toward home. The leaves are gone, nothing but bare branches crane over the car. I found this poem "One Art," by Elizabeth Bishop: *The art of losing isn't hard to master,* that's the first line. I've decided this is the Fall of Lost Things.

My mother and I have lost the ability to talk. It's as if the vacuum of Nani's absence sucks up every word we might speak. Sometimes, I catch her staring at me. She always smiles and turns away, goes back to whatever she's doing. My brain forms "I tried to save her," but it gets lost on the way to my lips, so I say nothing at all.

It's not just my mother. It was the same with my relatives in India. Aunts, uncles, cousins, everyone wanted to know about Nani. I vaguely recounted her last days, how she had gotten sick early. I told my relatives that she died without pain, without fear. I'm sure that's not true, but why tell the truth about death?

We get home, and Bapuji is awake with Preeti on the couch. Preeti has made it her goal in life to catch up on all the television she missed. She had programmed the DVR to record everything before we got locked down. While we were trapped, my parents kept every episode, recorded everything to DVD once the DVR was full, just in case, so that when Preeti got out, she'd have them all, wouldn't miss a minute.

Preeti's still very weak. She almost didn't come with us to India, but Ba didn't want to split us up, and she is a doctor, after all, so we made the trip as a family. Preeti spent the whole time lying on cushions, watching everyone run around in the garden. She pouted and whined. The mall seems to have changed very little about her.

"Good party?" my father asks.

"I saw Ryan," my mother says, smirking.

"Ah," my father says. "As much trouble as we thought he'd be?"

"He's very handsome," my mother says.

My father places his hands over his ears. "It's better that I don't know."

I smile because my father is trying to be funny. I wish I could tell them about Ryan. What he means to me. But it's more of a feeling than words. Instead, I say, "I'm going to take a shower," and begin mounting the stairs to the second floor.

"Again?" Preeti asks.

"Leave your sister alone," my mother says.

I've taken to showering several times a day. There's something delicious in being clean. I have a near constant desire to feel water running over my skin. When I'm not in the shower, I'm outside. My mother keeps yelling at me to put on a hat, that it's November and I'm going to freeze, but I love the way the breeze tickles my scalp, how the cold sends shivers through my body, the way the crisp air burns my lungs.

Once in the bathroom, I turn the water to hot and step into the stream. Mist envelops me. When I can't take any more heat, I turn the water to cool, then sit on the floor of the shower and let the rain fall down. As the steam dissipates, I see my story.

It came to me one night in Ahmedabad. I was lying

awake in my sleeping bag on the floor of my cousin's bedroom, watching patterns of headlights from the street below trace across her ceiling, and smelled a familiar smell. Following the scent, I found henna. There'd recently been a wedding of some other distant relation, and all the girls had been decorated with mehndi.

Bored, I took a bag from the pile. It was still moist. I began to draw on the top of my foot—just a mindless doodle, I thought. But it grew. The drawing circled my ankle. The waving lines curved into wings. They were my flight from the men who'd tried to hurt me. The wings became hands, the man's as he grabbed at me. Fingers forked up my calves.

It became my secret ritual. Every night, more of the story poured out of my fingers all over my skin. Bruises were encircled and inscribed with symbols: where they came from, when. My left hand was a lotus blossom, the palm, Nani's eyes.

Family members began to look at me funny. I ignored them. I hunched in front of a floor-length mirror on the bedroom wall and sketched curling smoke cut by beams of light across my lower back. Silhouettes of bodies crawled over the peaks of my hips.

My cousin Idaya, in whose room I was staying, interrupted me one night. "Are you okay?" she asked, yawning.

I was mid-drawing, working slowly around my belly button—a swirling pattern to capture that fluttery feeling I felt climbing with Ryan that first time. "I'm sorry," I said, dropping the bag.

"It's fine," she said, warily. "I have lots of henna. You're just kind of putting on a lot."

"I do it all the time at home," I said, trying to come up with some explanation that didn't involve my being insane.

"Oh."

"Nani let me use hers."

Idaya's eyes widened. "I'm so sorry," she said. She was my father's brother's daughter, not related to Nani.

I decided to use the excuse she gave me. "Thanks," I said. If she wanted to believe this was for Nani, that was fine. In a way, it was.

In the shower, water courses over my skin, adding patterns to patterns, glittering over parts of the story, bleeding them together. The earliest designs are fading. What's weird is that as the pictures go, so do the memories. I'm losing the feeling of that panicked run through the dark. I no longer taste the sour spit of that bastard who attacked me every time I close my mouth.

Everyone please move on, let fade the bruise.

The last design I traced was a repeat of the one I'd made that night before everything. The one Nani had feared revealing to my father, the one that drove us to the mall so early that Saturday. I finished it the night before the celebration of her life—the traditional calendar of mourning had been abandoned, seeing as Nani had been dead for so long, and there was no body to burn anyway.

I wore a loose white salwar kameez. The fabric was so fine that the red-brown of my henna story was visible to any who wished to look. When it was my turn to say something, I read a favorite Tagore poem of Nani's, one she'd read often after Nana's death.

*Peace, my heart, let the time for the parting
be sweet.*

Let it not be a death but completeness.

Let love melt into memory and pain into songs.

*Let the flight through the sky end in the folding
of the wings over the nest.*

*Let the last touch of your hands be gentle like
the flower of the night.*

*Stand still, O Beautiful End, for a moment, and
say your last words in silence.*

*I bow to you and hold up my lamp to light you
on your way.*

I step out of the shower and am confronted with myself. I had wanted to show this skin to Ryan, had wanted to take him to a room and just throw off my clothes as a test: Would he know the secret meaning? But I don't need to test Ryan. And more, I see now that no one could understand this story. That this is just for my eyes. That I told this story to myself.

We interrupt this program for breaking news.

My hand stretches out, finger points, and on the steam-shrouded glass of the mirror I scrawl: *We interrupt this program for breaking news.*

A knock on the door. "Shaila? That's long enough," my mother says. "The steam's fogging up the windows out here."

I turn off the water, open the door.

My mother is in the hall, placing towels in the linen closet.

"I wasn't there when she died," I say.

"What?" My mother jams another towel onto the shelf.

"Nani," I say. "I saw her after. There had been a riot,

and I got trampled by the crowds, and when I woke up, she was gone."

My mother gives the pile a hard shove with both hands. "Your nani, she could get all these towels in the closet. Even pushing with all my strength, I can't get them in."

I rest my fingers on my mother's arm. We haven't really touched that much since I got home, so we both look up, surprised at the contact.

"She rolled them," I say, taking out a towel. "That's how she got everything to fit." I unfold the towel, snap it straight, and roll it into a tube. It slides into a small crevice on top of my mother's pile, which threatens to avalanche onto the rug.

"Right," my mother says. "Yes. She rolled them. I remember."

"I want to tell you what happened," I say, "if you want to know."

My mother touches the hem of the rolled towel. "I've been trying to find the right way to ask, to talk to you. I was afraid if I said anything, it would be the wrong thing. How can I ask you to talk about such horrors?"

I take out the whole pile of towels and sit on the rug. "I want to tell you," I say, taking one from the top and beginning to roll. "It all started because of the henna tattoo, the one on my face."

By the time I'm finished talking, we've rolled all the towels, folded all the sheets, and fit everything neatly in the closet, just the way Nani always did.

My mother then touches my ankle. "And this?" she asks.

My eyes bloat. My throat contracts.

"You don't have to hide from me," she says.

And I'm back there, in the dark, eyes flashing in scraps of light, hands raking my skin. I can't tell her this.

"It's all I thought about," she says. "My two beautiful girls, trapped in that huge place, alone among thousands of strangers."

From the lines on her face, the shadows on thin skin, it's clear she was there with us every night in her mind.

The truth might be a kindness. So I tell her about the men. About Preeti, unearthed on the floor of a toilet stall. Even Ryan—there was some good in that place. I lay myself before her.

And when I have spewed the last horror, she holds me, the whole tangled mess of me, and whispers she loves me into the wet cords of my hair.

My mother and I are both somewhere between laughing and crying—snot running, mouths smiling—when Preeti comes up the stairs. Ba is telling the story of how Bapuji nearly got himself arrested after the FBI cut off our one CB conversation.

"He had his fists up like some cartoon boxer, ready to take on the entire army to get you girls back on the phone!"

Preeti is all snark. "Why are you sitting in the hallway?"

My mother reels her laughter back in, wipes her face with a washcloth retrieved from our neat honeycomb of terrycloth in the closet. "You should be in bed," she says.

"That's where I'm going," Preeti says.

"Then I'll come with you to tuck you in."

"Oh, god, Mom," she whines. "I'm not, like, five anymore."

But Preeti can't get enough of the attention. She even waits by the door to make sure Mom follows.

Ba squeezes my shoulder, and I rest my head against her arm. Then she meets Preeti at the door and hugs her thin shoulders. "You want me to read to you, or is that only for five-year-olds too?"

Preeti closes the door behind them.

I get up, suddenly aware that I am in the hallway naked save for a damp bath towel. It's still weird, going into my room. I'm not used to all the personal space, to sleeping alone in a real bed.

I throw on pajamas, then flip open my laptop. There's a new email from Kris, telling me the details for where he's going to pick me up on Monday. He offered me a job helping with his afterschool theater program. Of course I said yes.

I think about sending Ryan a message, but the words *breaking news* intrude. I try typing the line: *We interrupt this program for breaking news.* It doesn't feel right.

Digging through my desk, I find some loose-leaf and a pen. I write it over again. *We interrupt this program for breaking news.* The rhythm of the words pulses: *Da-dum-da-dum da-dum-dum da-dum da-dum.*

I think of "One Art," I think of the Fall of Lost Things. I think of Nani, of my painted body. And the words come.

We interrupt this program for breaking news:
The bad guys have been caught! It's finally over.
Everyone can move on, let fade the bruise.

How many died as part of their ruse?
Why count? This is the time for closure.
Don't interrupt our program to scavenge old news.

But I see remnants in the rubble: a hairband, shoes.
Why look? It's done. Spring will dress it in clover.
Everyone please move on, let fade our bruise.

I keep covering the wound, keep tightening the screws.
Push through each day. Maintain composure.
But what's breaking now is not the news.

Inside, the bomb ticks—all my effort, confused.
The inmates escape the wall of the enclosure:
Every one, please move on. Let fade my bruise.

I watch them spill out, spread, their power defused;
the lie was in the hiding, not the disclosure.
The world did not crumble after hearing my news.
Everyone can move on. Let fade the bruise.

My cell buzzes. It's one in the morning. My head throbs and my hand aches. It's a text from Ryan.

You didn't call.

I love that he's such a girl.

I text him back: *I was writing a poem.*

The phone vibrates and the screen changes to show he's calling me. I pick up.

"Will you read it to me?" he asks.

And I do.

L E X I

CHAT WITH D-MASTER

I'm going to be late today. Parental Unit has hair appointment.

Don't bother. Released early.

???!!!!

Don't blow a fuse. It's for my dad's memorial service.

Oh.
You want me to come?

It's going to be awful.

Obviously. You want me to come?

I'm going to be a mess.

You're always a mess.

Thx.

I don't want to go.
If I go, then he's really gone.

If you don't go, he's still gone. You just don't get to say good-bye.

Please come over.

When?

Now.

GINGER

"The cameras are going to be there, in the dining room," my dad says.

"But Deborah Winters, she'll be sitting with you here, by the fireplace," says a youngish woman named Kate from his firm. Kate moves around my house as if she lives here.

She and my dad are tag-team prepping me for my interview on *Night Chat* with Debbie Winters on cable. *Night Chat* was the only program that guaranteed my father could approve all questions and topics in advance. It's my first chance to tell "my side of the story"—Kate's words. But there's only one side to the story—the truth. And I don't need Kate to help me tell it.

"I have to get to school," I say.

"I can drive you," Kate says.

"I've got this," my dad says, touching her gently on the arm.

I leave the room to grab my bag from the kitchen table. "I'm going to be late," I bark over my shoulder.

On the ride to school, I flip through radio stations.

"Kate picked out a nice skirt for you for the interview," Dad says over a thumping pop song. It's one I haven't heard before. I've been gone long enough for there to be a new song-of-the-moment.

"I want to wear pants."

"A skirt looks more professional."

"Once people hear what I have to say, they won't care what I'm wearing."

"You can decide later." He doesn't say anything more until we get to the circular driveway in front of Irvington Country Day.

"You sure you want to go back today?" he asks. "We could go over things again for tonight."

"I'm sure."

He follows me out of the car so he can hug and kiss me good-bye. In front of everybody else who's getting dropped off. Like they don't already think I'm a wounded bunny.

We'll see who's a wounded bunny after tonight's interview. Once everyone knows how we were treated, how we were made to fend for ourselves, how people were jailed for no reason, left to die in the dark. I survived all that. No *bunny* could have survived all of that.

"Love you, sweetie," he says as I trudge across the lawn.

The door clangs shut behind me, echoing around the large vestibule of the side entrance, and tears spring into my eyes. As if by instinct, I am in the place where

Maddie and I have met every morning before homeroom since starting in the Upper School.

She's who I'm doing this for. Maddie and everyone else who died. The world has to know what happened to us. It can't all just be buried under tons of concrete.

"Hey, Ginger," some guy says, walking in through the doors behind me. "You're back."

"Hey, Liam," I say. "I am back."

"I watched it on the news," he says. "When they let the people out, and then when they blew the mall up. Crazy how they nuked the place."

"It's a crime is what it is," I say. "After what happened, to just bury everything like it doesn't matter."

"What was it like in there?" he asks, a smile creeping across his face. "Was it awesome, like some free-for-all? Or was it like the apocalypse with, like, dead bodies everywhere?"

"It was—" And suddenly my speech is gone. I had a whole thing planned out about the government's invasion, then how they left us, the senator's society. "At first—"

He raises an eyebrow. "At first what?"

"At first it was kind of— Well, see, I went there with Maddie. I mean, Maddie and I kind of always . . . "

The first bell rings.

"I have to go," Liam interrupts. "Talk to you later?"

He opens the inner door and swings it wide enough for the both of us. He trots away from me as if escaping a trap. Too bad Lexi isn't back yet to help take some of the pressure off. She texted that she might be feeling healthy enough to come back next week, but by then, everyone will already have heard the story from me.

I have to write my speech down, that's it. I'll get it down to a pithy punch line. *We were screwed by Big Brother.* That's a good place to start. I join the crowd in the hallway and find my locker.

Wrinkled wrapping paper, torn streamers, and deflated balloons cover its front. I can barely find the lock and handle under everything. There are get-well messages, like I was just home sick for a month. Someone made a collage with labels from my favorite stores. There's a picture of me and Maddie and some of the other girls we used to hang out with from the first day of school.

I tear it from its wrapping paper frame. Maddie's face is kind of hidden by Ariel's ponytail. It was windy. I remember having to keep holding my scarf down so Mrs. Yoshida could take the picture.

"Ginger!"

Hillary Kransfeld is running down the hall toward me, her brown bob flapping like a fringe around her hat, arms open, waiting to smash me into a hug. I brace myself for impact.

"Hi, Hill," I say into the thick knit of her head.

"Everyone's going to go insane when they hear you're back!" She holds my shoulders and smiles bright white teeth at me. "Oh my god, did you hear? No, you couldn't have. They're holding a service for Maddie today during last block."

"A service?"

"A remembrance thing. We're all saying something. We brought in pictures."

"Like this?" I hold up the one from my locker.

"Oh, we should add that one." Hillary pulls out her phone and begins swiping the screen with her fingers.

"We decorated your lockers, both of yours, right at the beginning, when we first heard you were in there. We all wanted to do something. It was so awful."

I have better pictures on my phone. Well, no. I guess I don't. My phone is somewhere in the rubble that was once the Shops at Stonecliff. Just another thing lost in the wreckage.

"You should say something about it," she says. "About what happened in there. Everyone's been talking about it, what it must have been like."

"I plan on it."

"I heard you're doing some TV interview?"

"Yeah. But that's only the first step. I want the world to know—"

"So what was it like? Was it crazy? I heard there were riots."

"Yes, but first it was actually—"

Hillary finishes whatever she was doing on her phone. "Were people, like, eating each other?" She looks hungry enough herself.

"No. I mean, in the beginning—"

"Oh, crap," she interrupts. "I should get to class." She hugs me again and runs down the hall.

Bells start ringing and I know I should go to class, but I don't even know what day it is in the schedule, so who knows what class I'm even supposed to go to.

"Ginger!" Ariel Blake waves to me from across the hall. As if reading my mind, she says, "It's a green day—we have bio together!"

Everyone's so excited to see me. I lope to Ariel's side.

"Thanks," I say. "It's weird coming back."

"Oh my god," she says, holding the door open for me.

"I can't even imagine. If you need to talk to someone, I am so here for you." She throws her arms around me. "I just had to do that," she says into my ear. "You know we all loved Maddie."

"Thanks," I say. But I'm a little uncomfortable with the line. No way did everyone love Maddie. Fear Maddie? Yes. Envy her? Sure. Maddie's thing was pissing people off. It's one of the things *I* loved about her.

Ariel lets me go and we walk into bio. My classmates jump from their chairs to greet me. They're all too friendly, too eager to not seem too eager. And they all say how sorry they are about Maddie. What did they have to do with it?

I thank everyone, give hugs, smile the way I'm supposed to.

After faking my way through bio, I follow the rush in the hallway to English. They're reading *Romeo and Juliet*. When I left, we had been on Book X of *The Odyssey*. Guess I'll never find out how that one ends.

Maddie had English with me. Her chair in the back is empty. She used to hurl her completely bizarre comments from that perch. *I think Odysseus is a punk—he's married to Penelope and she's, like, pining away for him while Odysseus is banging Circe. How is* he *the hero?* The teacher was totally dumbfounded. I bet no one in the class says stuff like that any more.

A kid I have never spoken more than five words to ever, turns around in his seat. "You have to tell me all about it," he says. His glasses give him bug eyes; in the mall, if he'd lost those, he'd have been blind, then dead. "Was it crazy? I heard the government was in hazmat suits Tasing people and stuff."

"There were people in hazmat suits."

The teacher tells him to sit straight and I'm rescued.

After English is my lunch period. I don't feel like eating, so I kind of hover in the administrative hallway, looking at the new artwork hung on the walls. It feels like I've been gone for centuries. There's even a new fad— people are wearing these cheap slap bracelets.

Now is the time to write down my speech for the interview. *The government has committed a crime against its people.* Ugh. That was Kate's line. And it's not even true. Okay, how about, *In the beginning, after the announcement, everything was actually pretty normal. Senator Ross tried to make things work. We had showers, jobs, clean clothes. We all ate together. Our biggest worry was whether we could sneak out to party.*

Should I mention the parties? It was my and Maddie's main focus. We planned our outfits down to the last bangle. I can't believe how much stuff we stole. All buried now. Gone. Poof.

I drift into World History and face another onslaught of inquiry into whether anyone tried to kill me for food. I say no. They don't deserve to know the truth.

The bell rings and it's announced that the memorial service for Madeline Flynn will begin in fifteen minutes in the Great Hall. We three—Lexi, Maddie, and me— were the only ones from our school in the mall, and only Maddie didn't make it out. I debate hiding in the library, but then Jenna Yoshida and Grace Bailey snag my arms.

"We will totally sit with you," Grace says in a voice like she's telling me I lost a leg, but I'm going to live.

"We made a slideshow," Jenna says. "Did Hillary tell you?"

"Yeah."

People are standing three deep against the wall. Everyone wants to be here for the memorial. Jenna elbows our way up to the front row, and so I am sitting with everyone's eyes boring into my spine.

First, the headmaster makes a little speech about lost friends and focusing on the good memories. Then the chaplain says a short, innocuous prayer. After that, the headmaster opens the floor to anyone who wants to speak.

Avery Dunmore gets up first. Avery hated Maddie.

"Madeline Flynn was the perfect example of what all students at Irvington Country Day should strive to be."

Is this girl serious? Maddie was like the definition of problem student. She was always one demerit away from expulsion.

Avery continues, "She was smart and funny and knew how to wear a studded belt with pearls. But whenever we think of Maddie, let's remember her amazing record-breaking season on the field hockey pitch."

Good god. If Maddie knew she was being remembered as a field hockey player, she'd start whipping people in the face with that studded belt. Each successive speech is worse than the last. Maddie was an excellent student. A super-great friend. Such a fashion plate. I'm not even sure who they're talking about anymore. It's like they're making the Maddie they always wanted, clipping pieces from the whole.

Jenna gets up with Hillary to introduce the slideshow. They have picked this totally cheesy song to play under it. People begin to weep. Some girl in the back mumbles along with the lyrics.

I cannot take this anymore.

"Are you people crazy?" I say, standing. "Do you even remember who we're talking about? Avery, didn't Maddie punch you in the face over the summer for saying something about her mom at Tomo's party?"

Avery's eyes scan the room nervously—she knows she's been caught.

"It's a memorial, Ging," Hillary says, giving me the stink eye. "We're here to talk about the good stuff."

"But this isn't the good stuff," I say. "The good stuff was Maddie punching Avery in the face for being a bitch. It was Maddie calling people out for being fake, for pushing us—for pushing *me* to be real, to be myself, always. Maddie was the girl who drank too much and set fire to people's lawns. She was also the one who got everyone dancing at a party.

"You know, it was Maddie who pulled the fire alarm in seventh grade. But she did it because she was trying to help distract people from the fact that I had gotten my period and bled through my jeans.

"That's the real Maddie. That's the Maddie I remember. She was smart, but she was no student. She was stylish, but only because she didn't give a crap about trends. She made the strangest things work as an outfit through sheer force of will."

Some people nod along.

"Maddie only played field hockey because she liked hitting things with sticks."

A few girls laugh.

"She was a great friend, but not in some Hallmark card way. She was my best friend, but not because she was easy. She pissed me off. She made me grow in ways I never would have on my own. She was braver than me. She taught me how to be brave."

A bunch of people clap. Some are crying.

"She was a great kisser," Josh Schiff says. A disturbing number of guys snicker and laugh.

The headmaster stands as if to scold them, but I jump onto my seat.

"Yes!" I say. "She loved to kiss boys!"

"All she ever wanted to do was play Truth or Dare," Samantha Ngo adds timidly.

"We played it in the mall!" I say, grateful that people are catching on, being honest. "She actually got the flu from it. I mean, even a deadly flu couldn't keep Maddie from hooking up."

"Now, Ginger, please," the headmaster begins, but people keep yelling out memories of Maddie's mischief. And she begins to materialize for me.

We had our eighth-grade formal in this hall. She wore this amazing blue dress. We went together stag, *To keep our options open,* Maddie said, but everyone knew it was because she and Brent had broken up the week before. We did each other's hair. I went nuts with the curling iron and she ended up with this massive knot on top of her head with a waterfall of ringlets cascading down her back. She ironed my hair straight, just for kicks. I'd never experienced straight hair before that night. It was so silky.

The bell rings, signaling the end of school. Everyone files out, but I stay in the Great Hall for a while, just to be with her. When I finally leave, I feel her presence in the hallways we've spent our whole lives running down. I pass her locker. It's the twin of my own. And when I get to the vestibule—*our vestibule,* as Mad would say every night getting off the phone, *See you in our vestibule*—I can almost feel her there. Maddie was always here before me— her mom dropped her off before heading into the city for work. She camped out on the top step in front of the inner set of doors, book and scrap of paper on her thighs, desperately trying to finish last night's homework, softly singing the wrong lyrics to whatever was playing on her iPod.

My breath catches on a sob.

She's really gone. Forever.

I feel so alone, it's like the air has been sucked from the space.

My dad is waiting for me outside. "Good to be back?" he asks.

I don't wipe my face, let the snot drip onto my scarf. "I miss Maddie."

"We all do," he says.

"You hated her," I say. "You thought she was a bad influence."

He glances over at me. "You all right, honey?"

"I just want to be honest."

The house is mobbed with vans and cars. Inside, it's a maze of wires and screens and chairs. Kate hands me my skirt outfit, and it's actually kind of cute.

"Thanks," I say.

She seems startled by the comment. "I thought it would look nice with your hair."

"I'm glad you've been here for my dad."

Now she's really taken aback. "Well, everyone at the firm—"

"You're seeing each other, right?"

"I'm not sure what your father—"

"I can tell," I say. "It's okay. My mom kind of abandoned us. It'll be nice to have a third for dinner."

She smiles. "I'd like to have dinner with you sometime."

Debbie Winters enters the house and we are introduced, and then seated in our chairs.

"You ready, sweetheart?" she asks me.

I nod.

She does her program intro, then the camera turns to me. "Ginger," Debbie says, "please tell us your story."

"I'm not going to tell you about the quarantine because honestly, I don't think you want to know what happened inside the mall. It didn't matter to you, not then. Out here, all you wanted to know was that you were safe. We kept you safe by staying inside. That's all you need to know."

I keep going before Debbie can interrupt. "The story I want to tell you is about my friend Madeline Flynn, who gave her life as a part of that plan, the one that kept you all healthy and alive. I want to let you know what was sacrificed to save you."

Even Debbie Winters knows better than to turn off the camera now.

L E X I

CHAT WITH D-MASTER

Can I ask you something?

You're sitting next to me.

Yeah, so?

I'm trying to watch a movie, here . . .

Is that a no?

You are the weirdest person on earth.

What do you think about me?

I think you wish you had my sniper skills.
I killed you last round in Ragnarok.

I mean as a person.

I'm going to punch you in the arm.

Ow.

This is totally meta.

I am trying to be serious here.

You are WEIRDING ME OUT.

If I kissed you, would that be a good thing?

What now?

You know, two people, with lips . . .

TYVM
How good a kisser are you?

Probably pretty terrible.

That's okay. We'll learn . . .

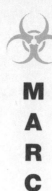

MARCO

The first day back at school, I caught myself spotting the exits from every room, identifying at least two things to make into a weapon. Ironic, because now I know my lifelong theory that I could get jumped at any moment was crap. No one gets jumped at school. It's always after, or elsewhere.

Besides, when half your face has been burned off and your hand shot through after surviving being quarantined in a death trap for a month, your average swinging dick is not going to mess with you.

Not only did school pose no threat for me, it held no interest. Just a teacher yapping at the front of the room—*Let's explore that question, Jimmy. What do you all think? I have a math problem coming at ya! In eighteen hundred and*—who gives a crap?

After surviving the apocalypse, what are you supposed to do with the rest of your life?

I stop at my locker to grab my coat. Out of the corner of my eye, I see Ryan. We've passed each other in the halls a couple of times. He raises his hand as if to wave. I slam my locker closed and get the hell out of there.

Outside, I stand close to the building, in the shadow, and close my jacket against the fresh air. When Mike's BMW pulls into the driveway in front of the school, I shoulder my backpack and take the steps two at a time to meet him.

"Nice day at school, son?" he asks. It's the same line every afternoon.

"Gee, Pop, I learned some real smart stuff!"

"You sound more authentic with every passing day."

"Kill me now."

He hits the gas and we just drive. There is no destination. New York becomes real country about a half hour north of West Nyack. Mike plugs in his iPod and we just go until the gas runs out, and then we fill the tank and go some more.

The album ends. I go to switch to another, but Mike tells me to hold on. He stops the car, then turns off the engine. It's six o'clock and already dark. The orange light of the dashboard throws shadows across our faces. It's the kind of light I like.

"My dad found this place in Arizona," Mike begins.

"You're moving?"

"For a little while," he says. "It's like a hospital." He looks out the windshield at the dark.

"Dude, if they are committing you, let's just go. Now. Hit the gas. We'll go to Chicago. Vegas. Wherever."

Mike snorts a laugh. "I'm committing myself."

I've got nothing.

Mike continues. "I'm not okay," he says. "I keep waking up and getting drunk and then passing out until I pick you up and then we just drive and all I want is to floor it off the Tappan Zee Bridge." His fingers are white against the wheel. "I don't want to feel like this anymore."

Mike glances at me. "Say something."

"What? That's great. Have fun. Send a postcard."

"I can't send anything while I'm there. No email, no phones. Just like the mall." He laughs like that's funny.

I keep my eyes glued on the dashboard.

"They have places around here too," he begins.

"Just take me home."

"You should talk to someone."

"Home, Jeeves," I say. "Just take me home."

We're way out in the middle of nowhere Dutchess County, so we're almost through *Siamese Dream* when we pull up at my house. "Sweet Sweet" is playing. How appropriate.

"I'll be back in a month," Mike says.

"Great."

"You don't have to be a dick about this."

"I don't?"

He reaches across me and opens the door. "Just take your little sad cloud self and go."

"Fine."

I snatch the top of my bag in my fist and haul ass. Mike guns it, slamming the door through acceleration and torque.

I will not cry over this bullshit.

The lights are on in my parents' apartment. My mom lost her job because she sat outside the stupid mall praying for miracles. I told her that was a waste of time. She thinks I lived because of her prayers. I told her I lived because I was willing to fight to survive.

"Oh, baby," she said, tearing up. "What did they do to you in there?"

I wanted to punch her face.

I sling the backpack over my shoulders and walk past my house. It's so cold my balls are freezing, but I keep going. I cross from my crappy side of town by the water up into the hills where the nice, rich people live. The houses are castles, so big, I could fit my family's apartment in them five times over. From the sidewalk, their blank faces look down on me, as if ready to send my ass packing should I loiter too long.

Screw these people. Screw everyone.

The wind picks up. The scar on my face tingles. It was warm in the mall. This cold feels like a personal insult. My parents allotted me a measly five grand out of the many thousands of dollars in settlement money the government forked over to spend on myself. I bought a leather duster. The government assholes took my other one. This one is nice, but the thin skin doesn't do crap against the cold.

I decide to hit a diner. The trek downhill is a hell of a lot faster than the one up, and in what feels like no time I'm in a plastic booth with some terrible, weak coffee staring at me. It's so easy to get food out here.

Everything is either too easy or too fucking hard.

"You order cheese fries?" the waitress asks. She's too

old for this job. Her eyeliner's bled down into the cracks around her eyes.

"Yeah."

She drops the plate on the table and moves on.

The bell on the door jingles and I hear girls laughing. Can anything ever be as funny as some girls' laughter makes it out to be?

"I still can't get over that thing you and Ariel did."

Lexi. Of all the diners in all the towns in all the world, she walks into mine.

"It was actually something Maddie had made up at a sleepover in like fourth grade."

I know this voice too.

"Well, whatever it was, it was funny. Best thing in the whole talent show."

They walk by me—well, the one girl walks and she pushes Lexi, who is in a wheelchair.

I can't make up my mind whether to say something.

"Marco?"

I look up from my fries. They both have stopped at the end of my booth.

"Hi," I manage.

Lexi is withered, but alive. Still alive.

"Don't look at me like that!" she says, flapping a hand. "I can walk. The wheelchair's just until I get my strength back."

"Oh. Good." I saved her. I did that.

"You hurt your face?" she asks.

"It's better than it looks." It looks bad enough that that has to be true.

The other girl has this weird smile on her face. "The last time I saw you, I was ready to kill you."

Now I know her. She was just on TV. Gave a totally bizarre interview about the quarantine.

"What held you back?"

"Her," she says, indicating Lexi.

Lexi blushes. "I hear you saved me."

I can't believe it. The girl told Lexi. "I owed you that much."

"It's not your fault that weird guy with the chicken kissed me."

She kissed Drew? Well, that clarifies everything.

"It's kind of my fault," I say.

Lexi shrugs. "I guess it kinda is."

I'm not sure what else to say. "You want to sit?"

Please, god, don't let them sit.

Lexi shakes her head. "We're meeting people."

"Oh."

The other girl—Ginger, that was her name—pops a hip. "Lexi's boyfriend. Darren. And some other people from school."

"Great." Like I needed to hear about Darren.

"It's good to see you," Lexi says as Ginger wheels her chair toward where the waitress left their menus.

"Yeah," I say.

I watch her roll away from me. She looks back once over her shoulder, gives me a smile, then turns away. The bell on the door rings again and there's more laughter and chatter as a ton of popular-looking kids in designer clothing fill Lexi's table to overflowing. A guy who looks kind of pale and nerdy, like he does not belong at all, strolls in. Lexi waves her arms like crazy. The guy's face lights up.

I leave a Hamilton on the table, shrug into my coat, shoulder my bag, and get the hell out of there.

It's gotten even colder, if that's possible. I watch the gaggle of people at Lexi's table through the window for a while anyway. They are silent on this side of the glass, a TV show on mute. Lexi looks happy.

I could go to a movie, or the Starbucks up the block, but it's late and I'm tired and freezing my ass off, so I just head downhill toward my apartment building. The central stairwell is filled with the sounds of the families on the lower floor, TVs blaring noise. I hop up the steps, then stop at my door to dig my keys from my bag.

"He's so sad," I hear my mother say.

No one answers, so I assume she's on the phone.

"He's your brother, *linda*," she says. "You should talk to him." She's talking to Gaby. Maybe they're planning to sue me.

I jangle the keys in the lock, then open the door and yell that I'm home. I hear my mother make her excuses to Gaby and get off the phone. She makes it a point to always greet me when I come in.

"Mijo," she says, wrapping her thick arms around me.

"You don't have to wait by the door for me," I say.

"I know." She lets go of me. "I want to wait for you."

"I just want you to know, I don't expect it."

"You never expect anything," she says. "You're a good boy like that. Not like Frida, ha! She would make a mess of this place, clothes everywhere! And did she think she had to clean it up? Never! You remember?"

The place was always a disaster when my sisters lived here. Dad had a better job, so Mom didn't have to work so many hours, but no one could have kept up with the mounds of laundry and dishes and junk mail.

"I was glad to have my own room."

"Well, you were the baby," she says. "You got special privileges. I made some *arroz con pollo* for your father to take with him. You want a plate?"

I don't want to piss her off, so I say yes. I'm actually kind of hungry. The cold just sucks energy out of you.

She watches me as I shovel the warm rice and chicken into my mouth. My mother is an amazing cook. I forgot how good her food was. With how much she'd been work- ing, she never had time to really cook. Now it's all she does. Clean house and wash clothes and cook. I don't like to admit how much I love it.

I scrape the plate clean, and she takes it and puts it in the sink.

"You want to watch a program?" she asks.

"Sure," I say.

We find some insipid sitcom. It's so mindless and formulaic, I can follow the storyline even as half asleep as I'm feeling. My mother chuckles where the writers wanted her to. It's really easy to make my mom laugh.

When it's over, my mother yawns. "I think I'll turn in," she says. "You?"

She has this hopeful look on her face. I guess she's noticed that I haven't been sleeping. I've been playing EVE late into the night, trying to claw my characters back from the hell my not playing for over a month sent them into. It's not even fun, but it's something to do.

"In a little bit," I say.

She nods, but looks like I just told her I was going to execute some puppies.

"I'll try to sleep," I add.

"Please try," she says. "We all love you. You know that, right, *mijo*? Everyone, we all love you so much."

For some reason, I'm crying. Thank god it's dark. My mother would lose it if she saw me crying.

There's nothing on TV, so I go to my room and open my laptop. There's a chat window open from where Mike and I were talking last night. I see he's online.

Check your tires, I write. *You left a trail of rubber an inch thick on the street outside my house.*

I thought you were going to say you knifed them.

I smile. *First thing on my list.*

You have a list now?

I'm writing one as we speak. First, knife Mike's tires. Second, find new ride.

Sorry, he says. *Hadn't thought about how I'm leaving you without wheels.*

I still have like three grand from the part of the settlement my parents gave me. I get my license next month. I'm thinking it'll buy me a sweet beater.

Maybe over Christmas you can test it out on Route 66.

Nurse Ratched allow visitors?

I'll drug her tea.

Then I'll be seeing you at the back entrance at dawn.

At dawn, then.

I close the laptop and stretch out on my bed. I'm still not used to luxuries like a pillow. Using my toes, I rake first one sock, then the other off my feet. I dig my way under my comforter, then lie flat on my back.

Out the window, the stars are brilliant. I tuck my hands behind my head and watch them shimmer as they streak across the sky. The next time I open my eyes, the clouds are pink and I smell sausage and coffee.

"You're going to miss the bus, Lazybones!" I hear my mother shout from the kitchen.

Holy crap. I slept.

"I'm coming!" I yell.

"Come faster!"

"Geez, woman. You told me to sleep, I slept!"

I jump out of bed and see that I'm still in clothes, so I just go out into the hall and make for the bathroom.

"Change your shirt," my mother says.

"Yeah, yeah," I say.

When I get into the kitchen—clean shirted with book bag packed—she has a plate ready for me.

"You comb that hair?" she asks, picking at my cowlick.

"Stop mothering me," I say, but we're both smiling. I don't know why, but I'm smiling.

I inhale the food, then jump up when I see the time.

"You home for dinner tonight?" she asks.

I could walk around again. But I guess I'll just come home. "Yeah." I go to put on the duster, but it was so cold yesterday, so I grab my old parka.

"Have a good day, *mijo*."

"Not possible," I say.

"I didn't say great day or exciting day. I said have a good day. Good is possible."

I climb onto the bus and see that my favorite spot is open. Not only that, but no one's giving me that hairy eyeball look I've been getting every other morning. I drop onto the seat and watch the world whip past and feel—for the first time in a long time—maybe she's right.

ACKNOWLEDGMENTS

Thank you first readers—Anne Cunningham, Mary-Beth McNulty, Matt Weiner, and Jennifer Decker—for your story insights and sharp eyes. And to Jamie Quatro for giving me some much needed late-stage input. Most of all, to my supportive, involved, insightful, and enthusiastic mom, Chris Kaufman.

Thank you experts—Karen Mangold, for keeping me honest in my medical misdeeds; my dad, John Kaufman, for teaching me how to ride a motorcycle; Cate Williamson and Alison Moncrief Bromage, for helping me write a poem; Jason for getting me to dig deep into the world of football; and to the local anonymous sources who helped me thoroughly trash my nice suburban mall.

Thank you to the team at Penguin Young Readers Group and Dial Books, including Don Weisberg, Jennifer Loja, Lauri Hornik, Erin Baber, Scottie Bowditch, Lisa Kelly, and Erin Dempsey, for all your support and enthusiasm for the series. And to Eileen Bishop Kreit and everyone at Puffin Books for putting out such beautiful paperback editions.

Thank you, Jessica Shoffel, for publicizing the series. Your kind words and guidance have helped me feel confident sharing my books and myself with the world.

Thank you to the design team behind these gorgeous books. Greg Stadnyk and Lindsey Andrews, you came up with another amazing cover. Jason Henry, I love how everything looks on the page!

Thank you, Regina Castillo, for lending your keen eyes once again to my words.

Thank you, Claire Evans, for making sure all the pieces came together, and for sending me good news.

Thank you, Kathy Dawson—more than thank you, bless you, truly. You push me to get things exactly right, ask the hard questions and point the way to solutions. You are everything I could have hoped for in an editor. I am so grateful to have had your brilliant mind guiding my work on this series.

Thank you, Faye Bender, agent and friend. You help me believe in myself on the days when that feels hardest.

Thank you, Evelyn, my dear girl, for being a constant source of joy and laughter. Thank you, Joshua, the new guy, for being adorable. And thank you, Jason, my love, for everything, but especially for being my friend.

ABOUT THE AUTHOR

Dayna Lorentz has an MFA in Creative Writing and Literature from Bennington College. She used to practice law, but is now a full-time writer and part-time cupcake enthusiast. She lives in South Burlington, Vermont, with her husband, two children, and two dogs.

YOU CAN VISIT DAYNA AT
www.daynalorentz.com
www.NoSafetyInNumbersBooks.com